To stay up to date on future books
by Michael Esola, please visit
www.PrehistoricMagazine.com

Unidentified

Michael Esola

PRIMAL PUBLISHING

ISBN: 978-1-7366738-3-6
Library of Congress Control Number: 2022912085
Primal Publishing
Pittsburg, Ca.

Cover design Copyright © 2022 Primal Publishing

Printed in the United States of America

Visit Michael Esola on the world wide web at www.PrehistoricMagazine.com

Dedication

"Master, master
Where's the dreams that I've been after?"

From the legendary album:

Master of Puppets by Metallica

PROLOGUE

The calm and placid waters of the South Pacific lapped gently at the shore. The rhythmic motion of the waves continued to come one after the other, constantly inundating the sand in a thin layer of glistening foam. The sun-drenched beach itself was deserted, the sand smooth and with almost zero imperfections, except for a few small bird footprints up near the part of the beach that headed back into the stands of trees, marking the sharp transition from beach into the dense jungle.

The start of the dark and entangled jungle some one hundred feet up from the water's edge was thick and lush; a stark contrast from the pristine white sand of the beach. Seagulls flew high in the clear sky and squawked loudly in protest to one another from time to time.

Meanwhile down below, dense stands of palm trees blew lazily back and forth in the warm tropical winds. From the blue turquoise waters to the near perfect white sand, to the lush tropical foliage, one could construe that this was truly paradise. A real Garden of Eden in the middle of the South Pacific.

A seagull dropped out of the sky and made a sharp descent for the powdery beach sand. Instead of landing on dry sand though, it opted for the thin layer of foamy water slowly trickling back down the sharp beach descent and toward the ocean. For a few seconds, the seagull's feet were completely inundated in the shallow water. But soon the water had made its way down the slope and back toward the ocean. Now the two small feet of the bird stood firmly atop wet sand, leaving its tiny toed footprints everywhere it walked.

For a brief moment, the seagull turned its attention back to the ocean, but more importantly the incoming waves. Quickly, it turned and with a few nimble and agile hops, made its way to a higher part of the beach. It watched as the wave crashed into the beach and the water ran up the slope and then stopped just several feet shy of its feet. It squawked loudly as the water slowly receded and made its way back toward the ocean.

And then, out of nowhere, everything died down around the seagull and came to a stop. Only the rustling of the palm trees further up the beach could be heard. The bird craned its neck around and stared back to the thick, impenetrable wall of palm trees. The bird continued to stare at the solid wall of trees before finally deciding it would go searching in some of the shallow pools of water that existed further down the beach. The gull had just hopped and turned its body around when there was an immense cracking sound from somewhere back deep within the jungle. It sounded like bulldozing or the obliteration of huge swaths of forest.

Several seconds of silence passed before the sound once again returned.

From deep within the trees, a distinct booming cracking sound rang out once again. The wet sand beneath the seagull's feet started to rumble and shake as though it were an earthquake. Although the seagull couldn't quite understand and comprehend what the sound of trees being cracked and obliterated actually meant, it knew one thing for certain; it heard these distinguishable noises before.

Completely entranced with these deep and unnerving noises from within the jungle, it had failed to recognize that a large wave snuck up from behind it. The water crashed down hard, completely inundating the beach now. The seagull quickly beat its wings several times and again lifted its body to a drier part of the beach. Quickly the bird craned its neck back toward the start of the trees.

The rumbling cracking sound like thunder rang out once again, but this time it came from much closer. Something massive appeared to be making its way through the trees and toward the water. The ground beneath the bird's feet rumbled and shook with untold fury now. The jungle was being annihilated and obliterated as something of unimaginable proportions was tearing a swath straight through the trees toward the water.

The bird beat its wings several times and lifted itself off the ground, agitated by what it could not understand. It knew that it needed to get away from here, needed to use its wings to soar high into the sky never to return to this place. Five more seconds passed before the bird beat its wings and lifted itself even higher into the air. Now it hovered some fifteen feet above the beach while squawking loudly. It continued on like this until finally the rumbling and cracking grew to such a loud decibel that it decided it best to get the hell out of there altogether. Thankfully, the winged animal had been given the gift of flight.

The earth rumbled and shook with an untold ferocity it had never known. And then suddenly out of nowhere, an enormous gust of wind swept violently through the area. There was an eerie force to its power, almost like the wind that follows an avalanche. These gale force winds blew over the top of the canopy as they headed toward the ocean.

Meanwhile the seagull, completely blindsided and caught off guard by this sudden windstorm, found itself struggling to get further airborne. Beating its wings furiously, the gull lifted itself high enough to get out of the powerful vortex that it had momentarily been thrust into. Suddenly the seagull noticed the oddest of sights. The sun had momentarily become blocked, almost as if a solar eclipse was taking place. A good portion of the canopy followed by the beach and surrounding ocean had also momentarily been blocked by what was essentially one long, continuous shadow.

***

With its colossal horned head towering close to three hundred feet above the forest floor, the monster thundered onward. Powered by its two enormous legs, the creature possessed the ability to go down on all fours if needed. Each step taken was as if a hurricane tore its way through the forest toward the beach. Trees and other low lying vegetation unfortunate enough to stand in its way were smashed and sent deep down into cavernous depressions in the earth. The entire jungle itself seemed to bow and cower in fear at the sight of the monstrosity.

Meanwhile down at the ground level on the forest floor, the jungle inhabitants fled furiously in all directions by foot or by wing.

Steamrolling onward and tearing a path of destruction straight for the beach, the building-sized creature opened its cavernous jaws and let loose an ungodly cry. The enormous bellowing sound rumbled from the great chest cavity and reverberated throughout the landscape. As another immense cry escaped the creature's gaping maws it was practically at the ocean now. Meanwhile, back behind it, the jungle looked as though entire areas had been stripped and clear cut—no vegetation, no growth, only destruction smashed flat in depressions in the form of enormous footprints.

With another deafening roar, the great chest cavity rumbled one final time and the creature bellowed a deep and resounding cry that pierced the earth. The monstrous feet of the beast broke free from the confines of the jungle, clearing the last row of trees with an enormous stride. The creature thundered into the shallows as water was splashed and displaced on all sides of the two gargantuan limbs. It lumbered its towering form several hundred feet out into the ocean. Now huge, towering waves fanned out on both sides of its mass as it pushed itself further and further out into the ocean, swimming and maneuvering its body like an enormous crocodile.

The monstrosity swam further and further out into the ocean with several flicks of its heavily muscled tail. Large patches of coral reef passed by below as huge gatherings of tropical fish and other marine life scattered furiously in all directions. Protruding out of the water, two enormous horns shot up from the sides of the skull.

And then with one final flick from the huge scaly tail, the creature submerged its great bulk, and disappeared into the murky depths below.

1

Forty-year-old Davis Brown readjusted himself from the driver's seat and let out a groan of agony. At just shy of six feet tall, he was built like a small tank, tipping the scales at a rock solid two hundred and twenty pounds. Fit with an athletic build, Davis sported close-cropped black hair up top and a light, neatly trimmed beard. He had come to America with his mother from the Philippines at a very young age. His father, a man of German descent, had run off with another woman when Davis was a toddler. This had forced him to grow up at a very young age, and over the years, had required him to do things for money that he wasn't proud of. But he was a survivor. And life was life. And you had to do whatever you had to do to get by.

Davis readjusted himself in the seat. His lower back and neck had seen better days though and seemed to only be getting worse with the passing of time. He set his hands down atop the steering wheel and looked out at the stagnant traffic. They hadn't even so much as budged an inch in damn near thirty minutes now. Davis looked over to his wife Elena who smiled back at him. She was barefoot and had both feet propped up on the dashboard and despite the fact that they were sitting in dead stop traffic on the Bay Bridge attempting to make their way into San Francisco, Elena had a rather relaxed and eased look about her. Whereas Davis was always tightly wound and under constant stress, Elena was a breath of fresh air, a cold glass of lemonade on a warm summer day. She was always cool, calm, and collected. He greatly appreciated this about her.

Elena Brown was in her early thirties. Tall and slender, she sported the fit body and frame of a runner. Her parents emigrated to the United States from Russia when she was just seven years old. Consequently, she had just the slightest hint of a Russian accent, but for the most part spoke near flawless English. Elena had shown a true passion and interest for music from a very young age. Her parents picked up on this instantly and not only encouraged her to pursue music but did all in their power to support her. Her love of music carried all through her schooling into high school and college as well. She studied classical music at the San Francisco Conservatory of Music with the ultimate goal of one day composing original film scores for feature-length films. She grew up worshipping and idolizing the great film composers of the past such as John Williams, Jerry Goldsmith, Hans Zimmer, James Horner, and Alan Silvestri to name a few. She hoped in time that she might actually get her chance to compose and conduct a score for a movie. So far though it remained an elusive goal. But she wasn't one to give up easily, and she felt as though if she kept her head down and focused in on honing her craft and building her skills, that her time would eventually come, that her ship would one day finally make landfall. It was only a matter of time, only a matter of time.

"You okay, babe?" Elena asked, looking over at her husband.

The two had been married for close to ten years now. At times it felt like it had been a long marriage, a mini eternity. Like all couples, they fought from time to time. But they always made up, always loved one another, and most importantly always fully supported each other's creative endeavors.

Davis continued wrapping his knuckles hard on the steering wheel for a moment before replying. "Yeah, I'm okay."

"Just okay," she said putting her hand on his knee. "We'll get there okay. Just relax, breathe, and most importantly take it easy."

Davis managed a smile as he turned and faced her. "In life or with this traffic?"

She smiled a big warm and inviting smile back to him. "Both."

"You're gonna make it in Hollywood," Davis said suddenly. "I just know it. Your time will come. Just gotta keep grinding, stay at it, stay hungry. But your time will come."

"I hope so," Elena said with another smile. "I really do."

But for the time being they were trapped in dead stop traffic. Davis let out another sigh as he let go of his death grip on the wheel. They hadn't budged in so long he decided it best to turn the engine off. He set the car in park, pulled the emergency brake, and removed the keys from the ignition. Forcing himself to relax now, he sat back in his seat. Naturally, his eyes looked in the rear-view mirror. He could see the kids. They were each bouncing in their seats and kicking the back of the chairs as though they were crammed for space on a plane flight.

Davis and Elena had two kids; an eight-year-old boy named Pedro and a five-year-old girl named Ariana. Both had been behaving for the better part of the drive, but still, kids were kids and as Davis continued to stare at them through the rearview mirror, he knew it was only a matter of time before shit eventually hit the ceiling.

"Gimme that," Ariana suddenly screamed as she reached over to Pedro.

Elena both hearing and seeing this was on it quickly though. "You two need to learn how to share. We've talked about this."

Davis returned his attention back to the dead stop wall-to-wall bridge traffic. He had forgotten what it felt like for the car to actually be in motion. He rested his head atop the steering wheel for a moment. It wasn't necessarily the traffic that was weighing him down. It was his law degree, or better yet, his lack thereof. He had failed last year on three attempts to pass the bar. Having always prided himself on his ability to constantly keep coming up with new products and ideas, he had set out with the ultimate goal of going into patent law, the branch of intellectual property law that deals with new inventions. For the time being though that was all going to have to be put on the back burner.

That's when he and his good buddy had the ambitious idea to start a podcast and subsequential YouTube channel to follow called *Bullshat*. They had a ton of ideas on how to build a brand, a real genuine following, from audio content, to a blog and official website, to their merch store, to even—

Suddenly, Davis popped his head back up and stopped tapping his forehead atop the steering wheel. For a moment he thought he was dreaming, thought he was imagining things. But as he rubbed his eyes and fully immersed himself back in the present, he saw that a few random people had gotten out of their cars and were walking on the bridge, weaving their way in and out of traffic.

"What the…" he mumbled to himself.

With the kids still squabbling and fighting in the backseat, Elena repositioned her body back in the seat and focused her attention on what currently held Davis' attention. She pressed herself up against the passenger window. "What are they doing?"

Davis shrugged his muscular shoulders. "Beats me. Maybe just a stretch break."

Elena raised an eyebrow to him. "A stretch break, really, on the bridge, in the middle of traffic?"

He laughed for a second. "Yeah, that does seem kinda crazy."

"But seriously," Elena said straightening herself in the seat while still staring out the window. "What in the hell is going on?"

"Maybe I should get out to investigate or something, have a look around," Davis said as he turned his body and faced the direction of the people walking through the traffic.

Before Elena could even respond though, Davis opened the door and quickly slipped outside. Now standing outside on the bridge, Davis proceeded forward a few paces before looking back to Elena through the front windshield. The two exchanged a brief glance for a moment while Davis motioned for her to lock the doors. She did just that as he heard the clicking sound.

Davis turned around and began to investigate. On both sides of him, scattered aimlessly about in between the rows of cars, people walked forward. To Davis the entire scene had a very surreal, almost detached feeling to it. The smell of smoke and ash hung heavy in the air as he trudged forward.

As he made his way, he couldn't quite shake that feeling that he was in a movie, completely devoid of reason and intuition, lacking a soul, lacking purpose, just moving forward as if he were in a vast herd of sheep.

Strength in numbers, he thought to himself as he rolled his eyes.

Davis didn't like or agree with that bullshit thought pattern one bit. Being a San Francisco Bay Area resident and watching the Golden State Warriors play in the NBA, he knew that to be their slogan, their catch phrase. And while he did root for the Warriors year in and year out, he absolutely despised that statement.

"Strength in fuckin' idiocy," he mumbled under his breath.

Davis had never been one to follow others, to follow the trends. Rather than follow, Davis had always been one to go against the grain, to march to his own beat. Yet now he found himself walking on the San Francisco-Oakland Bay Bridge following a bunch of random people whom he knew nothing about.

With no warning whatsoever, an immense sound blared intensely into his right ear. Immediately, a ringing and tingling vibration pierced his eardrum. Davis turned to see that a small car had honked at him, and from such a close proximity the sound had been deafening. His ears were ringing as he continued onward. Meanwhile, up ahead he could see that others had entered into the Yerba Buena Tunnel, a large tunnel that connects the two parts of the San Francisco-Oakland Bay Bridge to one another and which goes right through Yerba Buena Island itself.

Davis continued weaving his way through the cars until finally arriving at the tunnel. Now it almost seemed as though they had entered into a large cement cave of sorts. All sounds within it echoed and bounced off the steep cement walls. A car suddenly blared its horn loudly, sending the cavernous space into a cacophony of deafening noise. This prompted other cars to do the same. And for a brief moment, Davis found himself caught in a rising chorus of honking cars. In the cement tunnel, the noise of all those cars honking simultaneously together was absolutely deafening.

For a brief second, Davis thought about sprinting back to the car, but having come this far outside he was not one to give up. He put fingers in both ears and continued moving forward through the noise. Eventually, the chorus of honking cars came to a stop. Many of the cars that had given up entirely on the traffic, sat with the engines off and the car in park. Davis didn't blame them one bit with the rising cost of gas these days.

Davis could see the huge opening at the far end of the tunnel just up ahead. Bright light streamed down through the massive opening. All he needed to do was get himself there and he'd be back out on the main part of the bridge.

Davis heard more commotion. He could see that a man that had turned himself around from a ways away just up ahead was now running back into the tunnel. The frantic man was screaming and waving his arms like a lunatic. Although he was too far away and the cement acoustics of the place made discerning the man's words impossible, Davis could see that the man was clearly worked up into a frenzy.

As Davis' pace went from a brisk walk to that of jogging, he could see windows being rolled down. Heads were popping out of those windows in an attempt to gain clarity of what was going on. He found himself running at a swift pace, traveling down the left side of the tunnel, hugging closely to the huge cement wall.

Davis could hear the man shouting even louder now, his frantic words and screams bouncing and echoing off the walls. He watched as the man came to a halt, grabbed the hood of one of the cars, and immediately started conversing with the driver.

Now the driver and the panicked man were talking at rapid fire, their words coming out of their mouths at a million miles per hour. Still hugging tightly to the cement wall, Davis approached the situation with caution.

"You say you saw what?" the driver of the car shouted through the open window. "What?"

Meanwhile Davis continued inching closer and closer, until finally he brought himself to a stop some fifty feet away from the two. Davis eyed the man standing next to the car.

For a split second, he thought about going over to them to find out just what in hell all the fuss was about, but as he was now bathed in the bright light from the huge opening in the tunnel, he decided he'd just investigate firsthand himself. Davis quickly started up moving once again. Still hugging tightly to the cement wall on his left side, he continued to work his way past the dead-stop traffic in the lane closest to him. He exited the tunnel and spilled out into the bright beaming light.

For a moment, time itself stood still. He looked out ahead, saw what had to be at least a good one thousand feet of tightly packed cars all dead stop stretched out before him along the Bay Bridge, each of them not able to go anywhere on account of the gridlock. Now in a blaring cacophony of noise, it seemed as though each and every one of those cars blared their horns loudly for all it was worth.

And then finally Davis saw it. Momentarily blotting out the sun as well as a good portion of the skyline for that matter, an immense mountain of a figure continuing rising up from the water. As the towering figure rose higher and higher into the sky, massive cascading waterfalls of gushing water fell from all sides of the colossal body. Davis remained deathly still as his mind worked frantically, trying to process just what in the hell he was looking at.

Craning his neck back at an awkward angle, he felt as though a massive mountain had suddenly risen up from the cold waters beneath the Bay Bridge itself. With water still cascading and falling everywhere in great sheets, Davis was finally able to make out what appeared to be a head as big as a small house atop a body that was as massive as a building downtown.

Davis focused in on the head of the beast, the head itself easily as large if not larger than a house. He saw two immense horns protruding from both sides of the creature's head. It was difficult to judge size and scale from the distance he was at, but he estimated the two horns to be the size of small trees. They reminded him of the horns one might expect to see on a bull. For a brief moment he remembered about his son going off about one of the predatory dinosaurs from the past that had horns. He couldn't recall the name of that dinosaur. It didn't really matter though. Clearly what he was gazing at with both awe and terror certainly was no dinosaur, based on the staggering size alone.

Moving on down the giant creature's body, he eyed two enormous limbs stretched out in front of it. The creature was obviously standing in the water on its two giant back legs, but given the staggering length of the front two forelimbs Davis wondered to himself if this leviathan could walk on all fours if needed? Perhaps. He didn't know the answer to that question though.

And then suddenly the creature moved. The huge head lined with colossal horns swung downward in a great arc and eyed the tiny cars still sitting idle along the bridge. The creature let forth a bellowing snort as loud and intense as thunder itself. The terrifying sound reverberated out across the bridge, continuing to rumble for many seconds longer from deep within the beast's great chest cavity. This was surely no sound that anyone had ever experienced before in the flesh. It was a cry from some other world, some other place in time entirely, but it was right now with them, standing in the waters of the bay staring down at the bridge.

Davis remained frozen in place; his feet glued to the ground. He found it hard to breathe, hard to swallow. He felt a mixture of awe, bewilderment, and true terror coursing through his body. There was an eerie silence, an eerie calm, almost as if people were still trying to comprehend what their eyes were showing them.

And then that calm and placid nature erupted, suddenly bursting to life. The colossal jaws slowly parted ways and let loose a deep rumbling cry, something that seemed to harken back to a more primordial time in earth's history.

The immense, cavernous roar had been an absolutely deafening sound, rivaled in intensity only by a 747 jet as it screeches down the runway. And then just like that, it was as if the entire bridge had finally taken notice. A giant chorus of honking cars ensued.

Car engines revved, horns continued to honk, some cars even tried to move themselves to a position where they could drive up and out of here, but it was no use. The gridlocked, wall-to-wall bridge traffic wouldn't allow for it. Everyone was trapped for the time being. The tiny four-wheeled cars looked puny and almost comical as the creature raised an enormous, clawed front limb and gripped the side of the bridge, the impact jolting and shaking the bridge like an earthquake. The monstrosity gripped the bridge as though it were a toy to play with.

The image of Elena and his two kids in the backseat suddenly sprung Davis to life. Just before he was about to turn and head back to them, he caught one last fleeting glimpse of the colossal beast. At first, he thought his eyes were deceiving him, that he was seeing things. But as he stared for a few precious seconds longer, he realized that what he was seeing was no trick of the eye. Moving down one side of the creature's building sized mass, he saw what looked like small black dots traveling down the animal's body. Transfixed and unable to pull his eyes away from the sight, the skin of the monstrous creature had suddenly come alive.

Davis had absolutely no clue what to make of the horrific sight. Whatever the black dots were traveling down the side of the creature's body, one thing seemed apparent—they were headed straight for the bridge.

"What the fuck," Davis mumbled, stumbling forward several feet.

In one great big swath, Davis attempted to take it all in. He saw the giant head of the creature, the two horns protruding from both sides of the skull, the body itself as big as a building downtown. And last but not least, his eyes locked in on the shifting black shapes as they continued making their way down the creature's body, heading in the direction of the bridge. Davis took one last look at the giant creature and then focused back in on the moving shapes down the body. He knew one thing with relative certainty, that whatever this creature was, wherever it had come from, it now appeared that the moving black shapes were headed straight for the bridge.

Davis was just about ready to turn and head for the car, when he caught one final glimpse back to the creature as it reached out with an enormous limb and set it down heavily atop the bridge. Now there was absolutely no doubt that whatever it was crawling down its body had a limb to travel across in order to step off onto the bridge.

And with that he turned and began running, back toward their car, back toward his family.

Quickly, he ran, weaving his way through the traffic. Once back inside the tunnel, he was instantly bathed in the steady chorus of echoing honking horns. Davis ran full speed, hugging as tight as he could to the huge cement wall that lay on his right side. It had been a little bit of time since he had been in an all-out dead sprint like this, and it instantly took him back to his collegiate football days. Having played running back for a small Division 3 college nearly twenty years ago, his muscles still remembered what it felt like to run for his life against gargantuan football players much more massive and imposing than himself. It felt like he was once again running for his life, although this time he found himself running from a different enemy, a different force of nature. He probably had a good thousand feet back to the car, if not a bit longer. He kept his pace up.

Breathing hard and pumping his arms and legs for all they were worth, Davis exploded out the other end of the tunnel. Not a single car or person on this side of the tunnel more than likely had any knowledge as to the fact that a creature the size of a building was currently standing in the shallow waters of the bay. The huge tunnel and forest of trees that grew atop it blocked the view back to that part of the bridge.

Davis found himself momentarily disoriented. Breathing hard and winded he brought himself to a stop. Quickly he scanned the cars. It took a few seconds, but eventually he spotted their car. He sprinted toward it.

His mind spun in overdrive, working hard to try and comprehend and make sense of what he had just seen and witnessed. He was finally close enough to see Elena through the front windshield of their car. Davis arrived at the car, threw open the driver's side door, plopped himself down and into the seat, and locked all the doors.

For a moment he simply sat there with his head resting against the back of the seat eyes closed, sucking in ragged breaths as if he had just run the marathon of his life. He sat there for a few more seconds as he tried to regain his breath. He could hear Elena turn further in his direction and readjust herself in the seat.

"Well?" she said inquisitively. "Anything?"

Davis took a few more breaths as he tried desperately to compose himself. He grabbed the rear-view mirror, readjusted it so he could see their kids still seated safely in the backseat. He saw both his kids smile back at him. For a strange moment everything appeared to be good.

Davis let go of the mirror and shifted in his seat toward Elena. The two had been married long enough for her to know instantly when something wasn't right. And right now her senses were screaming at her telling her that something was indeed not right.

"There's, there's, somethin' out there," Davis finally managed to get out, looking his wife square in the eyes.

"What do you mean something?" she instantly replied.

When there was no initial response from him, the kids decided to speak up from the backseat.

"What is it, Daddy?" Ariana asked in an inquisitive voice.

There was no response from Davis though.

"Yeah, Dad, c'mon," Pedro said. "What is it? What's out there?"

"Well?" Elena asked shrugging her shoulders.

He set his hands atop the steering wheel and peered through the windshield for a moment. "I don't know."

"What do you mean you don't know," Elena said, her voice was now beginning to grow a bit impatient.

"I don't know what it is," Davis finally said. "It almost doesn't seem real whatever it is, like I imagined the whole damn thing."

"Babe," Elena said reaching out and grabbing his shoulder. "What is it? What the hell's going on out there?"

"A creature of sorts, an aberration seemingly ripped straight from the depths of hell itself emerged on the right side of the bride out of the water not more than five minutes ago. I, uh, still can't believe it. Hard to process it."

Elena's first reaction was to giggle quietly to herself. Even the kids got a good kick out of what their dad had just relayed to them. Davis had to admit that even by his own accord, the words that had just come out of his mouth sounded preposterous.

"Coooooool," Pedro said in a long and drawn out tone. "A real-life *Jurassic Park* brought back to life."

Pedro Brown, along with legions of other kids his age had grown up utterly fascinated with dinosaurs. The release of *Jurassic World* in 2015 and *Jurassic World: Fallen Kingdom* in 2018 had only served to further cement that love for all things prehistoric. He had grown up imagining worlds that existed eons before man finally arrived on the scene, to mess things up completely, to literally destroy the earth.

Davis looked to their kids and then back to Elena. His own worried expression must have been quite evident because his wife, seeing into his eyes, now had the same sense of worry on hers.

Again, Elena grabbed Davis by the shoulders. "Babe, what is it?"

He shook his head staring straight ahead. "I don't know. It...it was taller than the bridge itself."

She shook her head in disbelief. "What was taller than the bridge? I'm now following."

"The creature, Mom," Ariana said still giggling from the backseat. "The creature. I bet it was one of those creatures with big huge scary teeth."

Elena didn't even have a chance to follow up with another question before out of nowhere a deep and immense sound rang out. At first it was hard to place, hard to make out just what the noise could have been, but as Davis quickly rolled his driver's side window down, it sounded like the bending and screeching of metal.

"What the?" Davis mumbled to himself while still hanging his head out the window.

But instead of stopping, the grinding and screeching sound of metal only continued to get louder, more intense, more terrifying. The ground rumbled and shook beneath their car.

"What's going on?" Ariana screamed from the backseat. "Daddy?"

Davis suddenly shifted himself in the seat, his attention now focused squarely on the kids. "Everything's gonna be okay. Let's just try and calm down, okay."

But as the immense rumbling and screeching sound only continued to intensify in decibel, Davis knew damn well that something was terribly wrong. And then the grinding and screeching gave way to an immense roar.

Davis waited with his head still out the window as everything suddenly died down. Silence followed. He hung on for a few more seconds before finally opening the door quietly and stepping outside. The air carried a strange and foreign smell to it, almost as if something unimaginable or inconceivable had just happened.

***

The monstrous creature stood with its two enormous feet firmly entrenched in the soft mud and silt of the waters of the San Francisco Bay looking down at the tiny cars, making each and every one of them look comically small. It didn't know what to make of them, just that it thought very little for them. Rather its full attention was with the huge bridge that hung suspended in the air via the massive cables and supports. One enormous front clawed limb rested heavily atop those very supports and cables.

Meanwhile, beneath the gargantuan clawed limb, hundreds upon hundreds of cars continued to blare their horns loudly. Again, it paid no attention to them. The monster retracted its giant front limb. And for the briefest of moments, the creature took several steps backwards in the water. Giant waves formed on all sides of its colossal limbs as it continued to back itself up. And then it lowered its head, stretched its neck out, and blared a roar the likes of which no one had or would ever hear again. It charged forward through the shallow water, lifted its huge, right, clawed limb into the air, and then with an ungodly amount of force and ferocity, sent its immense hand crashing down through the bridge, tearing part of the bridge away as everything slowly collapsed and crumbled toward the water below.

***

Davis had heard every bit of the commotion followed by what sounded like a building collapsing and falling to the ground. His mind spun, running wild with worst case scenarios. He got himself back into the car and slammed the door shut.

Things were happening at rapid fire now, and he

knew they didn't have a moment to spare. And to make matters worse, both kids in the backseat started to scream and cry. Ariana was visibly upset. Pedro was holding out a little better, but still the small boy had a look of terror plastered squarely across his face.

Unbuckling her seatbelt, Elena maneuvered herself from the passenger seat so as to comfort both children. The intense rumbling continued on, the sound itself seeming as though it had been drawn up from the very core of the Earth itself.

By now Davis was uncertain what to do. He rolled the driver's side window down to try and gain clarity once again. Again, they heard an ear-splitting sound followed by what appeared to be the breaking and tearing of cement. It honestly sounded like the world was ending, and it was all happening just on the other side of the tunnel from where they were.

"It's gonna be okay," Davis shouted over the deafening rumble. "Just hang in there."

Davis realized that his words to his family had been meant for them as much as they were meant for himself. There was one last enormous booming sound and then just like that, nothing, no sounds at all. Only silence.

For a moment no one said a word. Davis and his small family sat there stunned in silence, each of them afraid to budge, afraid to move, afraid to breathe.

The silence stretched as Davis finally found the courage to once again hang his head and neck out the window. It was dead quiet outside on the bridge. The air was still thick and heavy with smoke. The fires up north in Napa were continuing to burn, but the air also had that dead quiet feel to it, like something wasn't quite right.

Davis eyed Elena out of the corner of his eye when

suddenly he spotted something from up ahead in the tunnel—a dark silhouette of a shape, moving fast. He reached to the glove compartment and grabbed his monocular. He brought them up to his eyes and peered through the lens. It took a moment for his eyes to focus. Immediately, he felt an elevation in his pulse coupled with his heart starting to beat faster. From what looked to be a ways back in the tunnel, he saw the dark shape moving swiftly between the cars now.

He managed to lift more of his body out of the window. He stared through the monocular back to the tunnel. The dark silhouette of a shape was still moving swiftly through the cars. And then suddenly it emerged from the tunnel and shot out into the light.

Davis felt the air momentarily taken from his lungs. He pulled his body back inside the car. Instantly, his mind harkened back to the sight of the monstrous beast as it stood looking down on the bridge just a few minutes ago. He thought back to the dark black shapes moving down the body of the massive beast. He vividly recalled seeing those black shapes traveling down one of the monstrous limbs of the beast, making their way for the bridge, almost as if they were going to—

All of a sudden, Davis felt the very ground beneath the car tingle and vibrate.

Elena spoke at just above a whisper now. "You feel that?"

Davis nodded his head as he carefully weighed their options for a precious second longer. "C'mon we can't stay here. We're getting outta here."

And with that he opened the door and made his way

outside. Wasting no time, he headed for the back door where Pedro was still buckled in.

Meanwhile, this sudden change in behavior had whipped Elena up into a furry. "I don't understand. What's—"

"We can't stay here, need to get outta here, possibly get to higher ground," Davis yelled back as he unbuckled Pedro.

Elena did the same to Ariana, and before any more protests could be rattled off, the small family of four stood huddled closely together on the bridge just outside their car.

"Where're we gonna go, this is crazy," Elena screamed.

Davis eyed the far-left side of the bridge now, the area just in front of where the start of the tunnel in fact began. That was a distinct part of the island that lay flush against the bridge. There was also a very steep grass hillside there as well. That's where they would go. That's where they needed to get to. And that's just where they headed.

With Pedro running close to his side and Ariana firmly secured in Elena's arm, the family of four took off toward the far-left side of the bridge, maneuvering their way through the cars. When they finally neared the cyclone fence that Davis had been eying all along, he managed to turn himself around one last time.

And what he saw rocked him to the very core. He witnessed a large creature suddenly come into focus. Surely this animal had to be one of those dark shapes traveling down one of the giant limbs of the massive building sized creature's body. Whatever it was, it towered high above one of the cars now. Davis saw a huge head lower itself down and over the hood of the car, and then with a quick burst of energy, one of its huge-elongated arms ending in razor sharp oversized claws shot forward and punctured straight through the glass of the windshield. The impact was so powerful it broke the entire windshield with one stunning blow. Now the panicked and screaming driver behind the steering wheel lay completely open and exposed. The immense creature pulled the screaming man from his seat up and into the gaping jaws.

There was a blood-curdling scream from deep within the huge mouth before the terrified cry cut off abruptly. This was followed by a sharp crunching sound, the crushing and pulverizing of bones. And then in one final act of aggression, the creature threw its big head back and swallowed the man down whole.

Davis had seen enough, and unfortunately so too had the kids.

"Holy crap," Pedro blurted out.

"Let's go," Davis called out.

They stood not more than fifty feet or so from where the creature had just emerged out of the tunnel and eaten the man.

Elena was already at the fence. "How do we do this?"

Davis set Pedro down on the ground. The minute he did so, the young boy couldn't help but look back to the carnage that they had just seen. Meanwhile, Davis connected both hands together and worked on hoisting Elena up and over the fence. She was a good athlete and in a matter of seconds landed on two feet on the other side. The second that her feet touched down on dirt marked the official transition from the bridge onto Yerba Buena Island.

Next, Davis grabbed hold of Ariana and went to

work placing her on the top of the fence.

"You can do it," he said to her.

Having spent quite a bit of time in gymnastics, she too was a good little athlete as well and had no problem climbing down the other side of the fence. When Davis went to reach for Pedro, he found his son had already started climbing.

"I got it, Dad, just worry about yourself."

Despite the urgent nature of the situation, Davis still found time to nod and smile to himself for a moment. Both of their kids were growing up way too fast. Together as one, father and son went about the task of scaling the cyclone fence. Quickly, they reached the top of the fence and then both of them jumped down and onto terra firma.

Just as they landed on the other side of the fence, a deep cavernous roar suddenly erupted over the steady chorus of cars blaring their horns. There were also cars ramming into one another in an attempt to escape the horrific beast, but there was ultimately no way to flee the wall-to-wall gridlock traffic. Davis took one last look back to the chaos ensuing on the bridge before finally turning and facing his family. "Let's go."

2

The big head of the juvenile creature towered close to twenty feet above the ground. Swinging left than right, the enormous creature suddenly took off in the direction of a pickup truck. From the back bed of the truck, a small shaggy object was yapping loudly. The ground tingled and shook with each step that the enormous animal took in its pursuit to get to the barking animal.

As the enormous apex predator drew nearer, it most certainly didn't know what to make of the small, yapping dog covered in long flowing hair in the back bed of the truck. All it knew was that it had identified this small animal as another potential food source. And in order to attain the staggering size of the adults, particularly that of its mother, the juveniles needed to constantly be feeding, constantly in search of their next meal. For this creature the dog was that next meal. The huge jaws lined with sharp oversized glistening teeth parted ways as the creature strode forward on two powerful limbs.

When it neared to within ten feet of the shaggy barking dog, there was a loud sound of a door opening and closing followed by the cocking of a shotgun. The big head swung in the direction of this new and foreign noise.

The huge predator looked down at the man dressed in jeans with a cowboy hat on. He was holding something long, slender, and black in his hands. He did something and again the object produced a sharp cocking sound.

***

The man who had just exited his truck was holding a shotgun aimed squarely at the towering beast now. And he fully intended to do all in his power to protect his furry four-legged companion. As the man came round from the front side of his truck, he honestly felt as though he were looking a living, breathing, T-Rex square in the eyes. The creature was shockingly large.

The massive predator lowered its head and blared a deafening roar aimed squarely at the man. The ground vibrated and shook beneath the man's feet as the huge thing lumbered forward, jaws open, exposing a huge array of sharp serrated teeth, the huge-clawed forelimbs outstretched, ready to pull him limb from limb.

The man held his ground though. When the creature took one more step forward, he fired with the shotgun. The deafening blast hit the monster somewhere in its great chest cavity, the heavily muscled animal taking the bullet almost like it was nothing. It was clear that the blast from the shotgun had absolutely enraged the beast.

The shot had done little to deter the determined carnivore though as it strode forward on two giant limbs. The big head lowered, the huge jaws parted ways, and the creature closed down tightly around the man's body. It was hard to tell whether another shot was fired or not, as within a matter of seconds the man was lifted clean off the ground and disappeared into the creature's gaping maw.

With a fearsome shake of its massive head back and forth the immense mouth closed shut tightly, the powerful jaw muscles working in unison as they pinned the body in place. Blood shot out both sides of the jaws as the sharp serrated teeth pierced through bone and flesh. The creature threw its head back even further now. And with a loud and distinct crunching sound, the cavernous jaws lined with huge, serrated teeth began to consume the man. What was left of the body was now traveling down the throat, headed straight for the giant belly of the beast, the great chest cavity. The creature let loose one final thunderous cry before sending its great bulk crashing off in the opposite direction.

3

The small family of four had heard every bit the commotion that had just played out in real time back on the bridge. From the sound of cars honking repeatedly, to the sound of cars ramming one another in an attempt to flee, to the sound of a shotgun going off several times, to several earth-shattering roars; all of it had played out in big, bold, and horrifying cinematic fashion. As they ran now, everything appeared to be permanently burned into each of their subconscious's. But worst of all, was the sound of the man's terrified screams as he was eaten alive. The scream had cut off abruptly. For a moment, Davis found himself caught in a reoccurring loop of what it would be like to be consumed alive, to be swooped up and off the ground by the jaws of death itself, and then to slowly watch those walls of massive teeth close shut on you like a tomb. Eternal darkness and death followed closely after. This was the fate of such an encounter.

As they ran, Davis hoped in time they would be able to unsee and unhear what they had all just witnessed. It was a near impossible task though. There are just some things in life that you just can't unsee. But worst of all was the fact that he was struggling with this as an adult.

He could only imagine the true terror and fright that must have been running through their children. What type of potential flashbacks and nightmares would they suffer from all of this?

They were traveling down a small gravel road now. A steep grass hillside dotted with towering eucalyptus trees lay at their right, and on that hillside lay several small white buildings. Davis quickly eyed them. All the windows on the lower level on both of the two small buildings were boarded shut as were the doors to both buildings as well. Whoever lived inside meant to personally see to it that no one was getting in or out. It most definitely felt appropriate given the current chaotic and unpredictable status of the world.

The four of them continued onward.

Suddenly Pedro looked up, staring at his dad straight in the eyes. "We're good, right Dad?"

There was zero hesitation in Davis' response. "We're good. Don't worry about what we just saw back there. We're gonna be fine. Everything's okay. Just keep movin'."

Davis suddenly reached down and swooped Pedro off the ground. The boy was surprisingly small and light for his age. Davis knew in time that his son would grow and bulk up, but for now he was quite a bit undersized. But his lack of size made him all the more manageable to carry. Davis was grateful for that.

Now with Pedro firmly secured in his arms, the two hurried on ahead toward Elena and Ariana. When she heard her husband's footsteps fast approaching, she managed to turn herself around despite still running hard. Seeing Pedro in Davis' arms, she did the same and instantly picked Ariana off the ground.

Now Davis and Elena were running top speed with both kids hugging tightly to their chests.

"Up there," Davis shouted, pointing to the base of a large tree. "Let's hole up there, take a breather."

Crossing a small street that divided the two forested hillsides from one another, they ran for another hundred feet or so before finally hunkering down and taking up shelter at the base of a massive eucalyptus tree. Elena was first to crouch down next to the huge tree. Ivy clung and grew so dense at the base of the tree that it actually allowed them to conceal and hide both kids in the thick growth. The two adults were too big to fit into the ivy however.

Davis and Elena sat huddled close to the concealed kids inside the ivy. Breathing hard, they did their best to take it all in. Things had been a blur, a mashing together of horrific sights and sounds. Davis could hardly comprehend the fact that they had left the confines of their car behind and had now found their way off the bridge and onto the small Yerba Buena Island.

It was hard to take it all in, it really was. But despite this and the feeling that this wasn't real, wasn't quite reality, Davis knew that he one hundred percent had to keep it together for his family. They needed him to be the leader here, to take charge. They were also all going to need each other now more than ever as well.

4

Bob Levin sat absolutely petrified and panicked stricken behind his steering wheel. He had just watched a short while ago as a family of four emerged from their car and headed for the fenced off area before finally climbing up and over the fence altogether. He had also witnessed something awe-inspiringly huge lunge straight for a man and eat him alive.

Even though it had only happened not more than ten minutes ago, these scenes were permanently burned into his memory. He vividly recalled cracking his window just enough to hear what was taking place back out on the bridge. He heard a monstrous roar that heralded the arrival of an apex predator the likes of which he thought only existed in big budget Hollywood blockbuster movies.

Bob felt his pulse increase as he broke out into a cold sweat just recalling the sound of the dog barking from the back of the truck. And then permanently burned into his subconscious was the sight of the massive silhouette of the creature as it emerged into plain view.

Bob remembered hearing a deep cavernous sound, like the intimidating throaty sounds walruses make. And then after that he recalled seeing the man with the cowboy hat on emerge swiftly from his truck brandishing a shotgun. With the barrel of the gun faced squarely at the massive creature, the man held his ground firm. A shot was fired into the thick and seemingly impenetrable hide of the beast. The creature took the bullet like it was nothing though. Bob still vividly recalled that sound of nothing as the bullet from the shotgun seemingly disappeared straight into the mass of the beast. Whatever the huge creature was, it almost seemed impervious to such trivial matters such as manmade weapons and ammunition. This creature appeared to have been forged and made in another time in Earth's history, perhaps even down in the Earth's crust where molten and magma reigned supreme.

By now Bob's senses had reached a tipping point. Sweat formed atop his head and was now running down both sides of his face in tiny streams. He sucked in a deep breath of some much-needed air. It was hot and suffocating inside the car, and for a second, he felt as though he was going to pass out. He swore both sides of the car were literally closing in on him. Seemingly out of options, he opened his car door and stepped outside and onto the bridge for some fresh air.

The minute that his feet touched down on the ground he realized just how bad the air quality had once again become. The air was chocked heavily with the smell of burning embers, the direct result of the heavy fires that they had currently been experiencing in the northern California region for quite some time now. It felt as though anything with a dry grassy hillside and some trees was on fire and it honestly felt like they had all been thrust against their will into the bowels of hell itself.

The end of days, Bob thought to himself sadistically. *Could it actually be?*

He sucked in a huge breath of smoke-filled air in an attempt to get his oxygen-deprived brain working once again. The smoke burned deep into his nostrils and lungs. He drew in another huge breath, again choking on the bad air. It was as heavy and thick as he could remember in recent times. Life was consistently getting worse and worse with the passing of each year.

Feeling as though he was being watched from some unseen vantage point, Bob flung himself around wildly. Not certain what his next move should in fact be, his ears were suddenly assaulted with the harsh blare of cars honking their horns. The steady chorus of cars honking loudly surrounded him on all sides now.

Through the awful air and the thick smoke, Bob sort of staggered forward a bit. His left thigh slammed into the hood of a car. And the realization of where he was but more importantly where he was standing hit him full on.

Suddenly, his eyes twitched and made contact with the driver of the car. For the briefest of seconds both shared a deep and intense embrace. And then in a strange almost out of body experience, Bob Levin watched as the driver's eyes suddenly went wide with horror. From inside the muffled confines of the car, the man began waving his arms back and forth and screaming frantically. The only thing that Bob could actually make sense of was the fact that the driver was obviously trying to get his attention.

Before any further thought could be put into it, Bob felt the ground beneath his feet tingle and vibrate. Frantically he flung himself around. He had been spotted, marked for death. From a good hundred feet away and closing the distance quickly with huge strides, he watched as a massive shape came straight toward him. Bob could see the big head, overwhelmingly large chest cavity, the powerful tail behind the beast swinging and swishing in the air, meant to counterbalance the creature's colossal weight. And it was all steamrolling toward him like a moving freight train.

With great strides the young juvenile creature strode forward, powered by its two enormous legs built of sinew and muscle. Now one of the offspring of the giant creature that had attacked and destroyed the bridge rampaged forward through the cars in pursuit of its prey while unleashing a thunderous cry.

Bob Levin stood absolutely frozen in place, his feet glued to the ground, his body feeling incapable of movement at this point. He was frozen in fear, half not believing what his eyes were taking in. He felt like a deer caught in the headlights, and now the only way out of this nightmare appeared to be through a horrific death.

Somewhere in the far reaches of his brain, behind the utter fear of being killed and eaten alive, Bob knew he didn't have much time. He had to act quick. The sudden realization that an animal roughly the size of a bus was quickly coming his way forced him from his daze, forced his feet into action.

Bob turned around and took off running. He began making his way through the cars. It honestly felt like he was being hunted in the open ocean by a hungry shark. Quickly, he tried to locate his car. But in the madness of it all he had gotten himself turned around. Now panicked and running out of time, he couldn't spot it. There was no time though to further search for it. He could hear the creature and feel the ground as it drew nearer.

And then suddenly Bob remembered the family of four that had left the comfort and safety of their car behind and managed to successfully extricate themselves from the bridge entirely by going up and over the cyclone fence. That's just where he was headed now.

Breathing hard and out of options, he sprinted toward the fence. He knew the creature was close now as an awful wave of stench suddenly wafted his way. Eyeing the fence, he pushed his legs as fast as they would go.

Now the fifty-five-year-old man was running like he hadn't run in ages. As he closed to within fifteen feet of the cyclone fence, he could feel the cold fence within his grasp. He would climb to the top of it in a matter of seconds. And from there he would jump down onto the other side, hopefully to safety.

Bob reached out with outstretched arms. His fingers had just made contact with the fence when suddenly he was thrown hard up against it. The crushing blow from behind slammed his head and body into the fence, knocking the wind from his lungs. Immediately he found himself completely overwhelmed with a hot panting stinking breath. Still pinned up tightly against the fence, he felt scaly pebbled skin at the back of his neck. The creature exhaled sharply through its large, oval shaped nostrils, and Bob felt a stiff wave of rotten breath blow over the back of his neck. It was a sweet tangy nightmare that smelled of blood, meat, and entrails.

There was absolutely nothing Bob could do now as he remained pinned in place to the fence by the front of the creature's snout. It felt as though he was being held in place by the crushing force of a small car. There was that much power and strength behind the creature's big head.

And then all of a sudden Bob somehow managed to wiggle himself free. He slid awkwardly down the fence to the ground. Pushing himself off he took a moment as his feet scrambled to gain traction. He slipped and almost fell, yet somehow, he managed to catch himself on the fence. And then in a strange and detached part of his brain, his eyes took in blood on the ground, lots of it. The blood was splashed along the ground in great big splotches. That was his blood. In a quick flash he was suddenly thrust into a fiery and explosive world of pain. Unbelievable pain radiated outward from where the creature had slashed at him, cutting him across his back, and shredding his skin in long ragged claw marks.

Bob let loose a wet gurgled scream just as his body was lifted up and off the ground. He was lifted higher and higher into the air until finally he found himself inside of a huge gaping maw. He managed to see back into the throat of the creature, saw the large coiled lathered tongue covered in foam, saw the huge black opening at the back of the throat that led down to the depths of certain death itself. And then he saw the long coiled tongue lash out at him like a snake striking its prey.

The long-wet tongue held him with the intensity and pressure that a python grips and holds its prey with. Bob felt the tongue squeeze tighter now as it continued to wrap itself around him into tight coils. He could hardly breathe. As he exhaled another breath of air, he realized he suddenly couldn't breathe at all. The foamy tongue gripped him even tighter now. From inside the deep cavernous mouth, the sickening sound of bone cracking rang out.

Bob felt immense pain to his chest region as one his ribs cracked. The coiled tongue squeezed tighter, increasing its pressure around him. When breathing was no longer an option, two more of his ribs cracked and broke as the coils increased their pressure around him.

Bob was on the verge of unconsciousness as the lathery tongue continued to hold him in a tight suffocating embrace. And then all of a sudden, a huge wave of foul-smelling breath rose up from the back of the creature's throat and wafted his way. It smelled like a butcher shop, hell itself.

In a state of delirium that fell somewhere in between death and unconsciousness, Bob knew that his mind was rapidly failing him fast. But he had just enough brain power left in his oxygen starved brain left to process the fact that he was being eaten alive, to process the fact that this was really happening. Another wave of hot stinking breath rose up from the back of the creature's throat. Bob could feel that he was being dragged against his will deeper and deeper toward the back of the creature's throat.

As another hot breath of air struck him hard, survival seemed futile at this point. The wet, hot tongue of the creature had him wrapped in a tight embrace and would not let go deep within a cavernous mouth lined with massive serrated, curved teeth. What light did exist at the very front of the jaws now streamed in like light shining into a darkened cave.

It had all of a sudden become very silent. The air itself was hot and deathly still. A final wave of repulsive breath rose up from the back of the animal's throat. And in one great massive move, the creature threw its enormous head back. The top jaws closed down tightly, removing the last

41

of the available light that had been streaming in. And it was there, lodged deep in the jaws, wrapped and held in a suffocating embrace by the sharp serrated teeth and the wet and slippery tongue, that Bob Levin was pushed to the back of the throat, swallowed down, and sent to his final resting place.

5

The large black bear had been walking for quite some time now, making its way up and down the hard dirt hillside, foraging on berries and leaves wherever it could. Strewn everywhere across the hillside were thousands upon thousands of eucalyptus leaves that had fallen to the ground on account of the towering eucalyptus trees that grew in close proximity to one another across the hillside.

Suddenly the animal brought its wide girth to a stop. It had just finished making short work of a small blackberry patch at the very bottom of the hill. Now it was busy making the journey back up the hill in search of more of the delicious blackberries.

With the front of its snout stained with dark berry juice, the bear began the slow plodding journey back up the hill. A good hundred feet or so into its journey up the hillside, it spotted what it was in search of, a fresh new patch of blackberries. And by the looks of it, it was a good-sized patch of berries at that. The bear moved quicker now. It wouldn't be long before it was once again stripping the luscious blackberries from the branches by the dozens and gulping them down.

The trees and bushes off to the left suddenly shook with life. The bear brought itself to a stop. The big black head swung in the direction of the disturbance. As it did so, a gentle breeze blew down the hillside, rustled the leaves, and shook the low-lying vegetation. The bear stared for a while longer before the big head swung back around, allowing the four-hundred-pound creature to continue on its way up the hill.

The large animal had just begun moving once again, when suddenly the ground beneath its clawed feet started to rumble. An eerie moment of silence followed.

The bear remained frozen in place, stood deathly still.

And then from somewhere off to the left, there was an enormous explosion of leaves and limbs. The bear turned just in time to witness an impossibly huge creature emerge from the trees.

The black bear, completely caught off guard by this, immediately turned its bulk around and began charging down the hill. The four-hundred-pound bear got its body up to speed. From somewhere off to its right side, it felt an enormous fiery explosion of pain cut deep into its gut. The enormous predator tracking it had slashed at it with razor sharp claws. The bear howled in pain as it continued charging out of control down the hillside. As it bounded down the hill on four powerful limbs, out of the corner of one eye it saw a huge shadow materialize and cast itself over it.

The bear went to plant two front limbs down when, all of a sudden, it found itself tumbling down the hillside out of control. With no way to regain or stop itself, the bear quickly became a tumbling four-hundred-pound, out of control snowball.

The omnivore rolled end over end like this for another dozen feet or so before finally slamming hard into the base of a large tree. For a moment the bear simply lay there, its body crumpled like an accordion at the base of the tree. No sound, no movement.

And then with a great struggle, the bear slowly brought itself back to life. Planting its two limbs down on the ground, it lifted the front half of its body up, followed slowly by the back half. Groggily, the bear stood on four shaky limbs, dizzy and disoriented.

Painfully, the big head lifted itself to gain a better view back up the hillside. The moment that its vision came into focus, the bear froze right where it was. Charging full force down the hillside was by anyone's estimate a true nightmare of nature.

The young creature bellowed a rumbling cry that seemed to shake the hillside to its very core as it opened its huge set of jaws. Now the ground beneath the bear's limbs shook with an untold force. The bear doing the only thing it could, quickly turned and fled. But it was over before it even began. With another earth shattering roar the massive predator was upon the black bear. In pitiful protest, the bear swung its head in the direction of the charging creature and let loose its own combative moaning cry. The last thing that the bear saw was the huge jaws as they opened impossibly wide and closed shut over its body.

***

From just a ways up the hillside, Davis Brown and his family remained absolutely still at the base of one of the massive eucalyptus trees that grew on this part of the island. No one dared to budge an inch, dare to even breath for that matter. Davis and Elena had witnessed the horrific attack first-hand, seen the pure savagery, the sheer bloodshed. But the worst of all was the fact that their two small children had also heard the horrific scene as well. The sounds of ripping and tearing were more than likely enough to give them both nightmares until well into their teens.

Pedro and Ariana were still seated inside the confines of the ivy, hugging tight to the base of the tree while Davis and Elena were situated next to the thick ivy. These were tense and unnerving moments now, and as another stiff breeze blew down the hillside from above them, they were reminded that they were essentially still out in the open. The giant creature was probably a good two hundred feet or so away. They heard the breaking and the crunching of bones. And beyond that was the chilling sound of ribs cracking as the giant predator continued removing all traces of the bear's existence.

Quietly, Davis unhooked the monocular from around his neck and brought it up to his eye. He took a moment to focus in on the huge predator at the bottom of the hill. Immediately, he thought back to seeing the giant building-sized creature on the side of the bridge, but more importantly, to the dark shapes that had been traveling down the side of its body. Surely, this animal at the bottom of the hill was one of those dark shapes that had been working its way down the leviathan's body, diligently heading in the direction of the bridge. This must have been one of its young. There wasn't any other explanation that he could think of to describe just what it was he was looking at. But as Davis continued to peer through the monocular, it was hard to wrap one's head around the fact that the giant that stood before them was in fact a fraction of the size of the adult. Still, the creature feeding at the bottom of the hill was no less impressive, nonetheless.

Davis estimated it had to be close to fifty feet in length and stood damn near twenty feet tall. The weight, which was undoubtedly massive, was difficult to calculate. He watched as the predator leaned its bulk forward and went down on all fours. While it was clear that this animal walked and ran primarily on two legs, the oversized forelimbs allowed for it to spend time on all fours if needed. At least that was Davis' first initial impression of the animal.

Davis continued to watch as the predator pressed its long forelimbs into the carcass of the bear. The huge, sharp claws sunk down into the bear's fur. The weaponry that this animal possessed coupled with its staggering size just wasn't a fair fight. He eyed the two long, front, clawed forelimbs for a few further seconds. They appeared to be longer than a man was tall. He zoomed in closer with the monocular. The creature had thick tufts of hair that shot out from what appeared to be the middle of the long forelimbs. Davis zoomed out again with the monocular so he could take in the whole creature in its entirety. While much of the animal was a dark black, the underside of the huge gut and extending up the neck of the creature was a fiery orange. The top part of the huge skull was a dull gray, while the actual face and lower part of the jaw once again transitioned into that fiery orange color mixed with streaks of gray here and there. This colored pattern gave the animal a ferocious appearance.

Davis moved the monocular gently to have a better look. Shooting out the back of the head and extending their way down the neck were what appeared to be long, sharp, pointed quills. Davis' initial thought was that they reminded him of the quills of porcupines. The quills were very large though, possibly several feet in length. And they looked razor sharp to the touch. Moving on down the rest of the body, Davis saw the massive swollen gut. He wondered for a second just how much meat these things needed to consume? He then focused in on the huge tail meant to counterbalance the creature's great weight. As if this animal didn't have enough physical attributes, the long tail ended in four sharp spikes. Davis knew enough about dinosaurs from Pedro to realize that the tail of this beast reminded him of the spikes that Stegosaurus would have possessed on the end of its tail to ward off potential predators.

The sound of the creature chewing and ripping huge chunks of meat caused Davis to bring the monocular back around toward the head. He watched as the huge, bathtub-sized head lifted itself from the carcass and paused for a moment. Davis noticed shreds of flesh and meat hanging from the bloodied lower jaw. He could see that the creature also had two spectacular horns protruding out toward the top of its skull. They reminded him of the horns of a bull. Both horns looked very sharp to the touch.

As Davis zoomed back out one final time with the monocular, his mind was working at rapid fire, struggling to take in and comprehend this horrifying creature. Thick, strong hind limbs supported the animal's enormous weight. Razor sharp claws adorned both the toes and fingers of the creature. Davis' overall impression of this animal was that of a true apex predator at the very top of the food chain, with absolutely zero natural enemies.

Suddenly, Ariana appeared as though she wanted to sneeze. Davis was on it quickly though as he scooted himself forward and reached through the ivy and toward her mouth. He held his hand there for a few seconds as he suppressed the sneeze. When Ariana appeared as though the sneeze had completely subsided, Davis breathed a momentary sigh of relief.

In several large and commanding bites, they could hear the sharp, serrated teeth coupled with the great jaws which were anchored in place by tremendous muscles working in unison to reduce what had once been a four-hundred-pound bear to simply nothing at all.

For a moment Davis wondered how the bear had even got on this island in the first place. He knew that people lived here. There were homes on the island. Perhaps it had been a pet. Shaking his head, he didn't know the answer. These were strange almost apocalyptic times that the world was going through where anything seemed fair game. A distinct low rumbling growl called out from down the hillside. Still peering through the monocular, Davis watched as the creature lifted its towering head to its full height and surveyed the landscape. The big head swung left and then swung to the right. Davis knew one thing with certainty. He didn't want them getting any closer than this. This was already closer than he would have wanted them to be.

And for a brief, few seconds the towering animal stood completely still at the base of one of the huge eucalyptus trees. Again, Davis found himself trying to size the thing up.

He watched as the powerful neck lowered the big head and the creature once again continued to feed.

Davis had just unhooked the monocular from around his neck when just like that the creature picked up what was left of the bear in its crushing jaws and went crashing off and disappeared back into the brush.

All was deathly still.

For a moment, it was difficult to find the words to best describe what they had all just seen and witnessed. Finally, after several prolonged seconds of silence, it was Pedro who spoke up.

"Is it a dinosaur, Dad, because it sure as heck looks like a theropod, like a T-Rex or a monstrous Allosaurus. But the front two limbs are way too long, plus it has those two huge horns on its head."

The large animal that had just taken down and literally erased the existence of a four-hundred-pound bear in several aggressive mouthfuls appeared to be but a wee child, an infant, a juvenile. Davis was still completely enraptured with this thought. The idea that an animal that had to stretch damn near close to fifty feet in length, some twenty feet in height, and possibly weighed what two African elephants weighed combined, seemed completely absurd. Yet it all appeared to be true.

The response to Pedro's question finally came, although it had taken a little bit of time to get out. "No. It's not a dinosaur, son. It's something else entirely, not sure exactly what though, it just doesn't appear to be a dinosaur."

"Yeah, that sounds about right, Dad," Pedro whispered back. "Cuz dinosaurs went extinct sixty-five million years ago. Everyone knows that."

Davis smiled down at his son. "Not everyone knows that."

Pedro smirked. "Yeah they do, Dad, it was on the original Jurassic Park poster to the movie. It said, '*an adventure sixty-five million years in the making*'."

Both Elena and Davis managed to smile at their young son, impressed with his dinosaurian knowledge as well as his understanding of branding and marketing with regards to big budget Hollywood blockbuster movies.

***

While her parents may have been impressed with Pedro, Ariana however was not. She looked over at her older brother and simply stuck her tongue out at him. Pedro knew better than to say something back aloud though. Whatever it was that they had just seen would have given even the largest predatory dinosaur a run for their money in terms of overall size. He knew that for a fact. Despite only being eight years in age he had grown up on dinosaurs, *Jurassic Park* being his favorite. He preferred the original movie from 1993 to the more recent films though. Pedro liked the grittiness and rawness that the original *Jurassic Park* possessed. He liked the way in which the velociraptors were predators not to be messed with and avoided at all costs, as opposed to the more recent films such as *Jurassic World* which saw them as both friend and foe, running side by side along Chris Pratt on a motorcycle as he sped through jungle terrain.

After carefully deducing through some facts and figures in his head, Pedro now knew with relative certainty that what they had all just witnessed at the bottom of the hill was no dinosaur indeed. The arms were far too long, even allowing the creature to walk on four limbs if needed. Also, the immense jaws opened insanely wide. He knew of no dinosaur that could have opened their jaws to that degree. Running through a quick mental database in his brain turned up nothing. This was something brand new. But just what in the hell was it? While the overall body, primarily that of the two massive legs and the long muscular tail meant to counter-balance the great weight, supported the overall notion and appearance that it could have been a theropod dinosaur, the head and massive jaws looked like nothing he had ever seen before. Although he couldn't quite place it, the massive jaws had a sort of alien feel to it. Pedro wasn't certain where that feeling came from for him, just that it existed. Was this indeed some type of massive alien creature? He shook his head to himself. Again, he didn't know the answers to these questions, just that he believed with relative certainty that they weren't dealing with a dinosaur. He believed he could accurately say that now.

Pedro had just let out a slight sigh when he looked over to Ariana. She was still seated with her back pressed up tightly against the base of the tree. Pedro saw Ariana still making a silly face, sticking her tongue out at him while wiggling her small ears. He smiled back at her but didn't make a mean face or anything like that. There was a three year age gap between them, but at this stage in life the difference in age may as well have been a million years. Unlike eight-year-old Pedro Brown, five-year-old Ariana Brown was struggling to fully grasp and understand the true danger that she and her family were now in.

6

Thirty-one-year-old Matt Baker adjusted his Chicago Cubs baseball hat and continued on his way. In his right hand he had one of those high-tech walking poles. He'd bought the damn thing from REI roughly two years ago. Even though he had been slightly embarrassed to purchase the hiking pole in the first place, he had to admit that it had already aided his bad knees on several dozen hikes he had taken around the San Francisco Bay Area over the last few years. It provided him with stability and balance on treacherous, and at times difficult, terrain.

Having played baseball in high school as well as at a small community college back east, his knees had bore the brunt of all of that collegiate play. The catcher position had really done a number on his knees. Year after year of squatting behind home plate had made his body and primarily that of his legs much older than they in fact were. There was a lot of mileage on them, the same type of road mileage that had made San Francisco Giants catcher Buster Posey retire prematurely. Now it was simply about damage control and working with what his body would give him. The walking stick helped.

Matt had been busy hiking his way up and down these hillsides for the last hour or so in search of her. He brought himself to a stop, leaned his body up against the base of a eucalyptus tree, and pulled his water bottle from his back pocket. He drank thirstily from it for a few seconds longer.

His ears picked up on a bit of bird chatter from the outstretched limbs of the canopy high above. Matt craned his neck back to have a better look. Being an avid sports junky for the better part of his whole life, his girlfriend had stressed the idea of getting out and about doing more hikes lately. This is why he had moved to California from the East Coast a few years back, the favorable climate coupled with the fact that California offered the ability to go wine tasting in Napa one weekend, hiking in Yosemite National Park the next, followed up with either a Warriors or Giants game in the evening depending on whether it was basketball or baseball season. But he had to admit that living in the Bay Area things had become more complicated ever since the horrific fires of 2017 had set in place an annual August to late October fire season. The result of all these fires was bad air quality at certain times of the year. Right now was one of those times.

Matt let out a sigh to himself, took his hat off, and scratched his head for a moment. He had even gotten into birding as of late, again another recommendation by his girlfriend. He took in more of the birds a good hundred feet or so above him. Quite often lately he found himself envying them, their ability to literally take off at the drop of a hat and go anywhere they desired. They had the ultimate first-class ticket to go wherever they wanted simply with a flap of their wings.

Boy does that type of freedom sound good right about now, he thought to himself.

He ultimately knew that the type of freedom he was really talking about could only come from financial freedom, having that so called FU money. He was working on that as well, saving and investing diligently month after month.

Matt scratched his head some more before putting his baseball cap back on. He was going bald. It was a sad but true fact that more of his hair had already fallen out than still lay intact. And it was only getting worse. He suspected that sometime within the next year or so he would make the official decision to shave his head clean like a bowling ball. With that monumental task would come the ability to rebrand himself from a tired old teacher and youth sports coach into something far greater. Just what that far greater part was, he was not certain of at this exact moment in time. But he liked the idea of re-branding, starting anew, wiping the slate completely clean. He very much liked this new start approach. For far too long now he had looked like a tired old man with his balding mess of hair up top despite only being in his early thirties. It was time to start anew, start clean, start fresh. With a simple stroke of the razor, he would wipe the slate clean once and for all.

As Matt continued to lose himself with the local birdlife in the limbs and branches high above, he had grown momentarily distracted. This wasn't why he had come out here in the first place. Odd as it may have sounded, but several years back his girlfriend brought something small, furry, and black home to their Yerba Buena residence.

His girlfriend had brought the cuddly little creature home in a small wicker basket. Matt remembered approaching the basket with a bit of trepidation. Animals and pets had never been his type of thing.

He could still vividly recall looking down at the small black furry creature nestled gently in the basket. It took a moment but eventually he looked up at his girlfriend.

"Is that?"

She nodded with excitement. "It is."

Matt returned a confused look back down to the basket. "A black bear. You know we can't keep a bear. This is fuckin—"

The sound of a branch breaking from somewhere close by broke Matt Baker from his thoughts. Instantly he felt his body go into a heightened state of alert. He looked back up the hillside and just as he did so a stiff breeze blew down from above. It made a whistling sound as it whipped through the trees, rustling the leaves and limbs high above him.

He listened for a while longer and when no further noise came, he took two last sips of water before continuing on his way. As he began the slow and arduous trudge up the steep hillside, he was fully aware that their so-called pet had become literally too large to keep over the last several years. They had gotten the bear almost four years ago, and by now it had reached sexual maturity. And with sexual maturity meant that the creature was now tipping the scales at close to four hundred pounds. It had survived in their small yet rather isolated backyard here on Yerba Buena Island.

Consequently, they had been looking into getting rid of the bear well over a year ago, but then out of nowhere the pandemic hit and the world practically went to shit. There was also the idea that they had been raising and housing a bear illegally all these years to be fearful for as well.

With the aid of his high-tech REI walking stick, Matt struggled his way up the steep hard terrain that was this hillside. He had been carefully making his way, watching his footing with each step he took. The slick eucalyptus leaves that fell from the limbs high above and now littered the ground in spots made for a quick and easy fall. He simply couldn't afford such an accident.

Matt recalled the simple fact that they had wanted to give the bear away, and had gone to great lengths to find such a solution, but when the pandemic hit, they thought the task of finding a new owner for such a creature was indeed way too hard. They called it off on account of the current fucked up state of the world.

Matt came to a stop and looked around. He sucked in a few quick breaths as his lungs tried to recapture themselves. He also needed to get himself in better shape. All in due time though.

Fuck. That was damn near a year ago when we tried to give the bear away, he thought to himself.

Both he and his girlfriend had come to the decision that they'd simply keep the bear and wait until the world stopped ending to give the bear away. That had been their plan until one day the bear had simply outgrown their small backyard enclosure and broken loose via several old and rotted out pieces of fencing.

Another stiff wind blew down the hillside. Matt looked around, shook his head, and let out a sigh.

This is fuckin' crazy.

How this had even happened in the first place was beyond him.

"Why not get a dog," he mumbled to himself. "What's wrong with a dog? Who the fuck goes out and gets a bear?"

And then all of a sudden, out of nowhere he thought he noticed the tiniest of vibrations beneath his feet, almost like a small tremor in the earth. He looked down at the ground. He was in a combination of hard soil and loose eucalyptus leaves. He waited a few more seconds. He felt nothing. Perhaps he had imagined it.

Looking back up the hillside, he pushed his head down and continued trudging on. He hadn't gone more than another ten feet or so when suddenly a strong odor assailed his nostrils. The awful smell had literally come out of nowhere. Never having been one to shy away from offensive odors, Matt continued on though.

But he had to admit that even by his own estimates whatever the god-awful smell was, he felt as though it was one of the worst rotting, reeking odors that he had ever come upon in his life. He probably would have trudged on, probably would have made it to the very top of the hill, had it not been for the thick hordes of flies that had quickly overtaken the area.

Flies buzzed in and out and all throughout the bases of the huge trees. Matt was forced to take his Cubs hat off. He began swatting furiously at the flies. But when things became so thick, so dense, that swatting at lone flies was no longer a sound strategy, he began waving the hat furiously back and forth in front of his face.

Matt continued whipping his hat back and forth through a thick black buzzing mass of flies. When one finally flew in his mouth and he began to cough and choke, he had no choice but to bring himself to a stop.

Hunching over as if he were about to vomit, he coughed the dry heaves until finally he spat the small little fluttering black annoyance up.

Now that he had stopped moving, his sense of hearing once again took over. The mass of flies had a loud and steady drone to it. Matt had just taken in a deep breath of air through his nose when the smell once again hit him square in the face. This time, though, the intensity of that raw and putrid odor literally made him throw up in his mouth.

Matt decided that rather than go back down the hillside, he would take a more horizontal approach to things. Covering his nose and face with his baseball hat, he peeled hard to his left. He hadn't taken more than a dozen or so steps when he suddenly found himself getting entangled in a thick matting of undergrowth. In an attempt to lose the flies, he began moving faster through the low-lying shrubs.

He pulled his hat away from his face. He was going to need two eyes for this. In a matter of seconds, he found himself crashing through dense brush. He slammed through a thick layer of vines and ivy before arriving on the other side. Finally, having pushed through the last of the thick and entangled vegetation, Matt emerged out into a small clearing of sorts.

He could feel tiny pinpricks in the form of cuts and scrapes all over his body now. But he was happy to have left the thick matting of growth behind. Situated in the middle of the small clearing, the pungent odor hit his nostrils hard. It was like a punch square to the face.

Slowly, he started to take in the small clearing. To his surprise, off to his left he eyed another thick cloud of flies. Hundreds of them hovered close to what could only best be described as a grotesque mess. Matt stumbled forward as he tried to make sense of this. Again, he reached for his hat to cover his nose, mouth, and face with. When he neared to within ten feet of the buzzing black mass, he got his first good glimpse of it.

He moved closer. Through the mess of flies he saw long curved ribs. Red-pinkish meat still clung grotesquely to several of the ribs in certain spots. The entire image looked like some type of sadistic butcher shop. It was essentially one big pile of disassembled bones with the large rib cage in the middle of all of it. It was as though the large animal had ripped apart limb from limb by something even bigger.

He took in the familiar look of pale white bone. And then he realized those curved ribs were part of a much larger rib cage. Things were starting to come into clearer focus as he moved forward a few more feet.

Moving in a left to right sweep, he saw the rest of the huge chest cavity. His eyes locked in on the long and powerful neck still partially covered in thick and shaggy hair. The fur of the neck of the animal was matted down and slick with blood. Matt felt his pulse accelerate as he realized that the head and neck of the animal had been ripped apart and lay detached from the rest of the pile of bones. The final kicker came at long last when he saw the head of the bear caved and smashed in, lying on the ground in a growing pool of blood. The mouth was contorted, the jaws locked firmly in place in what could only best be described as one last dying agonizing cry. Matt was starting to get a better understanding of this creature's last terrifying moments on this earth. And it wasn't a pretty picture.

His pulse shot through the roof, his breaths coming in short but aggressive gulps. Matt looked back to the ribcage and then back to the caved in head still lying in a pool of blood.

He finally found the courage to speak. "What in God's name?"

He backed himself up several steps now. Out of nowhere, another stiff breeze blew through the trees and rustled the leaves. Terrified, Matt spun around. He saw the thick wall of vegetation that would lead him out of this small clearing and back to his original positioning on the hillside. All he had to do was push his way through it and he would put this place far in his rearview mirror.

Quickly he turned himself back around. Whatever the jumbled mess of bones was, most certainly didn't resemble the bear that he and his girlfriend had raised since infancy. But as he again looked back to the outstretched mouth, the mouth and jaws stretching out as if in one final howling moan of pain, Matt came to the sunken realization that this was their bear. How had this happened, but more importantly, what on God's Earth could have inflicted such damage upon the bear? He wasn't certain he wanted to find out first-hand.

Had it not been for the impending sense of doom currently pulsing its way through his body, he knew he would have felt tremendous sadness for the bear, their black bear, the one they had raised since it first came to them in that small wicker basket all those years ago. Matt's intuition told him that he needed to get out of this clearing, that he was potentially in grave danger. He had to get himself off the hillside and back to safety. Then and only then would he allow himself to breathe a momentary sigh of relief. As for right now, the only thing his mind and body were telling him was to get the hell out of here. It wasn't safe here.

His ears picked up on movement, noise, the sound of branches cracking and snapping from just beyond the thick wall of foliage. Something appeared to be moving out there. He waited and listened.

The clearing fell silent for a few seconds. The sound of movement picked back up once again just as he took one last look back to the revolting pile of bones. And with that he turned and eyed the route through the vegetation that had led him into this clearing in the first place. He took off moving in that direction. Giving little regard for life or limb, he plunged headfirst back into the thick growth. Plowing full steam ahead, branches and thorns from vines tore at him from all sides. But there was no stopping him now as he pushed further and further through the solid walls of vegetation.

As he continued on through the thick and entangled growth, movement from somewhere close by once again returned. It sounded like something immense turned itself around and had now taken notice of the small disturbance he was causing in his frantic pursuit to get back out onto the open part of the hillside. Matt moved faster now, pushed himself harder, as a sharp branch tore at the bottom of his chin and part way down his neck. He knew with certainty he was bleeding all over, but at this point he had no choice but to just keep moving forward.

Deep and unnerving cracking sounds confirmed what Matt had feared all along. He had been spotted.

Now the forest that stood just to the left of him came alive with the sounds of something tearing a path of destruction straight for him. Matt's mind instantly shot back to the aggressive and violent manner in which the bear's ribs and body for that matter appeared to have been pulled apart. Surely whatever it was moving just off to the left had been the culprit. But what type of beast could have done this to a bear that weighed in at around four hundred pounds?

He shuddered just thinking about such a creature. Matt had just pushed through a thick layer of ivy and leaves when suddenly he felt a slight vibration to the ground.

Holy shit.

But Matt just kept plowing his way forward. When he had to climb his way over a large branch that lay on the ground, he realized he wasn't tracking the same way back. He hadn't noticed a large tree limb in the middle of his way in here.

All paths lead to Rome though, he thought to himself as he made his way through another thick layer of vines.

Matt could feel the long draping ivy hanging down from the limbs high above. For a moment he found himself completely engulfed and entangled in ivy. And then with one great big surge of adrenaline he finally emerged out into the open.

He sucked in a huge breath of air, forcing it deep and all the way down and into his lungs. For a second there it almost felt like he was drowning in vegetation, had literally been swallowed alive by the sheer density of it.

Matt had just taken in another deep breath when an ungodly wave of foul-smelling air stopped him dead in his tracks. Scanning frantically back and forth for signs of life, again he felt the ground beneath his feet move.

He turned in the direction of the patch of vegetation that led back toward the clearing. Again, the sound of branches breaking and cracking put his legs into gear as he started backtracking down the hillside. More breaking, more snapping followed. He kept himself in motion though. He needed to put as much distance between himself and the approaching noise as possible.

Matt Baker watched as the leaves and limbs suddenly erupted to life as an enormous shape emerged from the trees. The large animal came bursting forth, roaring a gaping roar for all to hear. The bottom of his mouth dropped open while his brain struggled to make sense of what he was seeing.

A creature, with a head the size of a man and that stood on legs as big around as small tree trunks came bursting forth from the foliage. Matt watched as the big head lifted to its full towering height of damn near twenty feet above the ground. The creature produced a deep rumbling sound as the massive jaws parted ever so slightly, partially revealing the huge teeth that lay concealed inside. It reminded him of the deep guttural sounds that walruses are capable of. The towering creature took one more step forward, carefully eyed the man, and then with one final terrifying shriek of a cry, shot forward on its two powerful legs in pursuit of the retreating man.

7

"What is it, Dad?" Pedro whispered while looking up at his father. "What do you think it is?"

Davis honestly had no logical explanation for what they had just witnessed. He knew one thing for certain though, that if their young son who was a self-proclaimed dinosaur expert had no clue just what the hell these things were, then he was truly at a loss for words. He had no clue what these creatures were or how they even came to be in the first place. It was becoming more and more apparent that the earth had many more secrets to be unlocked than previously thought.

For a second, Davis thought back to one of the books he read as a kid. *Journey to the Center of the Earth* by Jules Verne had hypothesized that residing deep within the Earth's crust was a primordial world of creatures that existed hidden far away from the prying eyes of man. Could it be that there actually was merit to the story? Had these horrific beasts come from somewhere deep within the center of the Earth and managed to somehow find their way out? He shook his head quietly to himself. Again, he didn't know the answers to any of these questions. None of it made sense as far as he was concerned. Absolutely none of it.

"It sure as heck looks like a theropod dinosaur to me," Pedro whispered as he spoke up once again. "One of the big predatory dinosaurs from the Earth's past, like Carcharodontosaurus, Giganotosaurus, Mapusaurus, Tyrannotitan, or even T-Rex. But the forearms are much longer and the head is completely different, the jaws open way to wide. The thing is different."

Davis nodded. "Agreed."

From somewhere close by, a terrifying cry rang out. Several seconds passed before another monstrous roar responded. But this new rumbling cry appeared to have come from another location. This could only mean one thing. And it was a terrifying thought indeed.

"There's more than one of these things," Pedro whispered, almost in half shock, half disbelief.

The idea that there was more than one of these horrific beasts stalking and roaming the island was beyond a terrifying thought. It was downright chilling thought, but appeared to make total sense. After all, Davis vividly recalled seeing many tiny black shapes traveling down the body of the monstrosity that had come out of the San Francisco Bay and bore down upon the helpless bridge.

As Davis continued to stretch more of that memory, another bellowing roar rumbled out across the landscape.

How many of these things could there be? Davis thought quietly to himself as a wave of panic started to wash over him. He was doing his best to keep calm, keep it together, for himself as well as his family, but still at this point his mind was working at a million miles per hour.

The idea that there could be perhaps upwards of a dozen or so of these things roaming about on the island was beyond frightening. Seeing the creatures moving down the colossal wall of muscle that was the monstrous building-sized creature seemed akin to watching people mountain climb on the face of a mountain in Yosemite National Park. The idea that from afar a full-grown adult hugging up tightly to the face of a giant mountain such as Half Dome could look like tiny dots, it was the same type of reasoning that made the tiny dots atop the towering creature's back look like ants moving about the surface. But when those dark moving shapes finally stepped off the giant body and made landfall on the bridge, Davis and just about everyone else could see them for what they truly were—monstrous creatures in their own right that would have rivaled if not exceeded even the largest of the predatory dinosaurs from the prehistoric past.

Davis' head continued to swirl as he did his best to try and make sense of things. It appeared as though Pedro's observations were correct. Whatever these things were, they did not appear to be dinosaurian in nature. The overall size of the monstrosity that rose-up from the cold depths of the water on the right side of the bridge was far too large to have been a dinosaur. Davis had spent enough time with Pedro watching movies and documentaries over the years to know that no dinosaur had ever attained a size like what he had seen. In fact, now that he thought further about it, he realized that no animal on Earth was that big, not even the blue whale. Whatever the creature was that had risen up out of the water only to tower over the bridge as if it were but a child's toy, was on a scale the likes of which no documented animal on Earth had ever achieved. The implications to such a creature being alive were as breathtaking as they were terrifying, and upon formal documentation would not only set the scientific world ablaze, but the entire world for that matter.

But, as awe inspiringly huge as the giant monstrosity was, there was currently a more pressing issue at hand. They now had to contend and deal with the offspring of this creature; no easy feat in its own right. And Davis had already gotten enough of an up close and personal view of them to realize just how large and formidable they truly were.

"What about shelter?" Elena finally said as she broke the silence.

Davis managed a smile back at her. "Let's check out the building that we just saw a ways back."

Elena nodded back to him, already in the process of helping their daughter to her feet. Davis did the same with Pedro. The two kids' heads barely peeked above the vegetation line. To Davis it was a deeply unnerving feeling to be up and about once again, a terrifying reminder as to their newfound reality. The possibility that they were being stalked and hunted at any given minute was very much a grim reality from here on out.

"Let's go," Davis said quietly, ducking down as low as he could while grabbing Pedro by the hand.

Keeping low to the ground, the family of four began navigating their way through the dense shrubs before finally spilling back out into the open. Now fully out of the cover of the shrubs and bushes they felt completely naked and exposed. Davis could see the large two-story white building. They took off moving up the hillside in that direction.

Smoke had once again completely engulfed the hillside and filled the small island with unhealthy breathing conditions. Each of them donned their masks on as they ran. Davis could feel it deep from within. There was an impending feeling of gray doom. The sky above them looked dark, as soot and ashes continued to rain down in fine particles. There appeared to be no letup in the fires way up north in Napa and Santa Rosa. To Davis things had now taken on a post-apocalyptic feeling. The world was devoid of color, the backdrop at least for the moment was permanently a hazy gray in coloration. Things had taken on a very surreal and detached feeling as he struggled to make sense of everything.

"There it is," Davis breathed beneath his mask as the building finally came into full view.

As they pulled to within a hundred feet or so of the two-story building, Davis got his first good glimpse of the structure. Painted an old and rather dilapidated white in color, the building's overall appearance screamed of years of neglect. The building, for the most part, had seen better days. But it was a building nonetheless, and with that came the possibility of protection. They had no choice but to further investigate.

On the first level, where the windows and the door that led into the building were located, Davis saw nothing but boarded up wood. Whoever lived there had sealed the place up, windows, door and all. The family kept running, kept moving through the haze toward the building though.

Davis craned his neck back and eyed the second story of the building. He saw that each and every one of the windows up there were also boarded up. But then out of the corner of his eye, he caught something. A rather large window at the far-right side of the building that for some reason or another had not been boarded up.

Davis eyed the open and unobstructed window as they neared the building. "Maybe we can find someone to—"

The distinct cocking sound of a shotgun greeted them. And before Davis could put any more thought into the building, the barrel of a shotgun could be seen hanging out of the open window.

Davis wasted no time as he put his hands out and immediately brought his young family to a stop. Rather quickly, both he and Elena put their bodies in front of their two kids so as to completely shield them.

Looking back up to the window, Davis couldn't make out much of a face, rather just the dark black barrel of the shotgun which was now aimed squarely at them.

Davis got right to it. "We need help. Please. We're stranded out here."

"Too bad. Not my problem," a deep booming voice fired back immediately.

Quickly, Davis scanned the entire area as well as the small road that they had just traversed across to get here. For the moment he saw no visible signs of life. But he knew that things could take a turn for the worst in a matter of seconds. That was the stark reality they were all facing now. They had to keep their wits about them. "Please. We're in grave danger down here. Some type of horrific creature just killed a full-grown, four-hundred-pound black bear as though it were nothing. Please. We need your help or run the risk of not getting off this island alive."

"Again, not my problem," the deep booming voice

fired back. "Now get off the property or I'm afraid I'll have to use this thing. I don't want to, but I've got no qualms about using this thing if needed."

Davis felt the blood starting to boil inside him like a cauldron. He was absolutely enraged that whoever this coward was on the second story of the building, that the man appeared as though he would not lend a helping hand to a man and woman who had two small children and were in serious need of help.

Davis paused for a moment, swallowing what saliva had built up in the back of his throat. There was that anger and aggression problem that he and Elena had spoken about time and time again. The energy surging through his body now was like a coal burning bright. But he needed to control himself, needed to keep things together.

Davis tried his best to regather and compose himself. Rather quickly he switched it up and tried a different approach. "If you won't take all four of us, then please at least take my wife and two children and shelter them. Will you do that for me please?"

The man behind the barrel of the shotgun scoffed at the question, almost as if it were beneath him to give in to such a request. "I don't discriminate; young or old doesn't matter to me. Now I'm not asking you folks, I'm tellin' ya'll to get the fuck off my property. That's all I'm gonna say on this matter."

Davis took a deep breath, shook his head several times, and stared down at the ground. Again, he was doing his best to compose himself, to remain calm, cool, and collected. He took another deep breath in through his nose and let it out slowly through his mouth. Very carefully he stepped to the side and pulled Elena behind him. Now he was shielding his wife and kids from the man's shotgun. He stood between them and harm's way as the adrenaline continued to flow through his body like a river.

He felt ready to go, ready to brawl if the moment called for it. He held both fists clenched tightly at his sides as he worked on breathing in the air deeply into his lungs and letting it out gently. He repeated this a few more times before he felt the more rational part of his brain slowly starting to come back to life, the part of his brain that was hopefully going to get them safely off this island.

While continuing to make eye contact with the gun, Davis reached back and grabbed Elena's hand. She squeezed his hand for a moment for all it was worth. The simple act was enough to calm Davis' nerves. While there was no denying the fact that he wanted nothing more than to tear limb from limb whoever this piece of shit on the second story of the building hiding behind the shotgun was, he fully understood what Elena had meant by the simple gesture.

Davis was just about to put his attention back toward the barrel of the shotgun when suddenly from somewhere off in the distance they heard a soft rumbling. He froze, stopped breathing as he held the air in his lungs. An uncomfortable tense few seconds of silence passed by. The silence of the moment was shattered by the sound of the shotgun going off. The blast had come from the second level of the building.

From somewhere off a ways deeper in the trees that bordered the back part of the building, an enormous thundering roar rang out as if almost in direct response to the shot that had just been fired.

Davis turned quickly and looked back to Elena. "We

gotta get the hell outta here. Now."

"Agreed," she fired back.

For a precious few seconds, Davis looked around, trying to get his bearings straight.

"How about we try to get back to the car?" Elena finally said, her voice quivering as the words came out.

Another deep booming roar rang out from somewhere back within the confines of the trees. This was followed by the cracking and breaking of branches. Something immense was moving about in there.

Davis felt his body tense and tighten up on him. "Let's go."

Davis shot one more-fierce glare back toward where the barrel of the shotgun still hung out the open window. And then together husband and wife turned with both kids and took off running as the sharp crack of the shotgun rang out from behind them. They headed up a dirt path lined with weeds. Davis knew from prior times driving across the bridge that this path would lead them back to the bridge. They were headed back toward the cyclone fencing that bordered the bridge. Maybe Elena was right, maybe they needed to get back to their car after all. Perhaps that was all the safety they needed. Thoughts started to swirl in Davis' mind now at rapid fire.

Meanwhile, Davis kept looking up the dirt path, kept wondering when things would flatten out a bit and they'd see the fencing that bordered this portion of the bridge. Finally at long last he saw it. The traffic was still dead stop, no movement whatsoever. And then he felt his heart skip a beat as the silhouette of three enormous shapes suddenly emerged from just beyond the other side of the fence.

Davis saw them, each equally enormous in their own

right, dark black silhouettes against the metallic gray colored cyclone fence. These creatures appeared to be noticeably larger than the previous ones they'd already seen and encountered. Heads towered what had to be more than twenty feet above the ground, long thick muscular tails stretched out behind their huge-colossal bodies. And what was even more frightening was that this appeared to be a pack of them. Davis shuddered just thinking about a pack of these things working in unison together.

Suddenly from deep within one of the huge beasts, a terrifying rumbling sound bellowed out from the giant chest cavity. It was a frightening sound, a scream that seemed to echo from another world entirely.

Davis watched as the big heads suddenly swung in their direction.

"Stop," Davis whispered to his family holding out both arms wide, impeding anyone's progress forward.

Now Davis stood with his family directly behind him, again standing in harm's way between them and danger. Davis stood there, close to six feet in height and a solid two hundred and twenty pounds in weight against a small pack of creatures that combined together must have weighed damn near sixty thousand pounds. All that tonnage of solid rippling muscle perched on huge powerful legs stood just on the other side of the flimsy cyclone fence. The fence seemed pitiful in the presence of such monstrosities.

There was an eerie silent manner in which the huge creatures stood there frozen in place, the big heads completely motionless as the long powerful tails swayed back and forth rhythmically. Davis remained motionless as he just stood there with his arms hanging limp at his sides.

And for a brief moment, time itself stood still as all three creatures continued to stare silently back at the small family of four.

"What'll we do?" Elena breathed from behind.

Davis took a moment to further assess things before finally whispering back to her out of the corner of his mouth. "Maybe we can just quietly backtrack our way back down the path. Slowly, one step at a time. We should also lower our heads so as not to come off as a threat."

No sooner had the words left Davis' mouth when Pedro began to do just that. Quietly and unassumingly, the young boy began taking small steps backward just as his dad had instructed them to do. Elena and Ariana followed suit as well. Davis took a moment to linger behind for a second. With a calm yet calculated intensity about him, he eyed the three hulking behemoths standing just on the other side of the fence.

Davis held his gaze on the creatures for a few seconds longer before finally breaking eye contact. Slowly, he lowered his head toward the ground and began backtracking in the direction of his family. And together the family of four continued their way down the dirt path, moving slowly, heads down, putting some much-needed distance in between themselves and the pack of carnivores.

Progress was slow. Davis didn't want any sudden movement to startle the three creatures back on the bridge into action. They had probably gotten themselves a good fifty feet down the path when Davis heard what he had feared all along. Movement. Still backtracking, he carefully raised his head up just to the point where he could make out the cyclone fence.

His worst fears had indeed been confirmed. He

watched as one of the towering creatures extended its head and neck out over the small fence. With the massive jaws slightly agape, the long, clawed forelimbs of the creature began to pull back on the fence. The pitiful thing appeared ready to topple to the ground at any second like a flimsy house of cards.

Like a drug injected straight into the bloodstream, Davis felt a sudden rush of adrenaline. He had seen the strength of these animals first-hand. They had the ability to topple the fence to the ground if they so desired to. And if they ever got off the bridge and officially made landfall, there would be nothing on this planet that could stop them. They would outcompete, out hunt, and just plain dominate every animal species that walked and made its living on this earth. There was no denying this simple fact. Davis knew the chilling reality that nothing like this had roamed the planet since the time of the dinosaurs. He suspected at least for the moment that the sheer wall to wall gridlock on this portion of the bridge that led into Oakland and the San Francisco East Bay was keeping them in check. With the other section of the bridge that led into San Francisco now destroyed, the only option for food sources left Yerba Buena Island. For now though all they could do was to keep putting distance in between themselves and this pack of hungry creatures.

Quietly, Davis lowered his head and continued backtracking his way down the path. From a short distance behind him, he could hear Pedro, Ariana, and Elena still doing the same thing. He kept one eye on the ground at his feet and out of the corner of the other eye, he maintained eye contact back to the three creatures. But for the most part he was doing his best to keep his head lowered in as nonthreatening of a manner as possible.

And then out of the corner of one eye, Davis watched in horror as one of the creatures reached out with its long, sharp, oversized claws and began to pull the fence back. He saw the terrifying animal as it brought its huge hind leg up into the air and sent it crashing straight down onto the fence. There was a sickening, wrenching, screeching sound of metal being collapsed and flattened to the ground by the thick black claws adorning the huge, manhole-sized foot. The cyclone fence fell straight to the ground, sending up a large plume of dirt and dust in the process. With the fence now down, this meant that there was no wall of separation in between themselves and the pack of creatures.

Davis felt his eyes go wide.

"We gotta go," he shouted quickly.

Davis watched as two of the enormous creatures walked right on over the downed fence. And then one of the creatures in the back let out an unearthly growl. With thunderous steps forward and great huge strides, both creatures out in front took off running.

Davis turned and swooped Pedro off the ground once again. Elena picked Ariana off the ground and together the family of four was back on the defensive, back on the run.

"Where to?" Elena screamed, the terror in her voice real at this point.

Quickly, Davis scanned as they ran. There honestly appeared to be no way out of this living nightmare.

The sharp sound of a shotgun going off cut loudly over the advancing pack of creatures. Without stopping,

Davis managed to turn both he and Pedro around. The deafening blast of another gunshot rang out from somewhere close by. Davis managed to steal another quick glance back to the pack of creatures. The blast from the shotgun momentarily diverted the pack's attention as they went stomping off in that direction. This gave Davis and his family the window of opportunity that they needed.

The four continued running down the path. In the far background they could hear the staccato of gunfire going off.

Bam. Bam. Bam.

Elena was out ahead now running full speed with Ariana. She managed to turn herself around.

"Where to?" she shouted over the gunfire.

Davis looked around. They desperately needed to find some place to take shelter. Anywhere was better than just being out in the open like this. Davis continued scanning. His frantic search turned up nothing though.

And then suddenly, out of the corner of one eye, he started to see people, faces, bodies dotting the landscape here and there. It was quickly becoming apparent that they weren't the only ones that had exited their cars and stepped off onto the island.

From somewhere off in the distance, the sound of a cavernous roar cried out. Now it seemed as though they were truly experiencing Darwin's survival of the fittest first-hand. It was every man, woman, and child for themselves, pure survival in its purest and rawest form.

From up ahead, Davis watched as Elena slowed a bit. She had run cross country in both high school and college, and even though she was now in her early thirties, she had hardly lost so much as a step. She reached out quickly with her right hand and pointed.

Davis did his best to eye whatever it was that had gotten his wife's attention. At first it was hard to make out. He had hardly even noticed it. But as he watched as Elena and Ariana banked hard to their left, he spotted it. Lying in a rather dense gathering of ferns was what appeared to be a rusted over metal roof to some sort of shed or something. The rusted thing was lying on its own in the ferns, propped up on one side against the remains of an old tree stump. Most importantly though, the metal roof appeared big enough to offer up some type of protection and cover.

Elena and Ariana arrived first. Quickly, Elena set Ariana down on the ground. Davis was literally seconds behind her. Father and son got down on their hands and knees and crawled inside as well. It was big enough to cover all of them. Propped up on one side by an old rotted out tree stump, light streamed in from their backsides as they crawled toward the middle of it. As Davis looked up at their new hiding spot, it did indeed appear to be the old roof of some sort of dilapidated and abandoned shed.

Now they sat huddled close together as the main bulk of the metal roof covered them from view. For the moment they heard nothing; no sounds of a shotgun in the background, no monstrous roars calling out. Davis could hear his heart pounding in his ears. Reaching out with his arms he pulled his family closer to him. He held them all tight to his chest now for all it was worth.

"We wait it out," he whispered.

"Daddy, what's going on?" Ariana whispered back to him.

Davis reached out and touched her hair for a moment. "We're gonna be okay, sweetie, just need to wait here for a bit, that's all. Don't worry."

Suddenly, he heard the sound of sniffling followed by tears. Elena had been fighting it back for quite some time, doing her best to compose herself, keep it together for the kids, but now a small onslaught of tears flowed down both sides of her face.

Fearing that they were making far too much noise, Davis reached out with his hand and placed it down atop Elena's. He held it there for a moment, doing all he could to comfort and soothe her for the moment.

Slowly but surely, it seemed to be working. The sniffling and crying finally stopped when again noise from back outside appeared to be moving toward them. Davis felt his muscles and body tighten up on him. He could have sworn he just felt a slight vibration to the ground.

They waited in silence. And again, the ground beneath them received a tiny jolt. Something huge was moving in their direction.

Davis swallowed down what saliva had built up in the back of his throat. Quietly, he brought his hand up to his mouth, motioning for all of them to be absolutely still, absolutely quiet.

Davis needed to take a quick look outside their makeshift shelter. He needed to see where one of the creatures was in relation to where they were. Maneuvering carefully beneath the large, rusted over metal roof, he got himself into the correct position. Slowly he moved forward toward the part of the metal that was propped up slightly on the old-rotted remains of the tree stump. Davis was down on his hands and knees now trying to pull his body free of the covering.

He had just managed to free both his head and neck when again the ground beneath him vibrated. The huge predator was very close now. He tensed and froze. A few long seconds passed before he once again found the courage to move. Sliding the rest of his body forward, he pulled himself free. Now he remained crouched near the opening, the part of the roof that was propped up on the old tree stump.

Davis turned and faced in the direction of the animal. He felt the blood drain from his body. And it was there in that moment that he truly got a glimpse of the sheer size and scale of just what they were up against. He saw the huge powerful hind limbs of the beast. Upon closer inspection, the forelimbs of the creature, each limb tipped with sharp oversized claws, were unnaturally long and powerful, giving the animal the ability to go down and walk on all fours when needed. The giant forelimbs had to be damn near close to the length of a full-grown man if not more. From where he remained crouched in hiding, Davis could see the thick but extremely flexible neck. And housed atop that thick and flexible neck was the huge head, longer than a man was tall. The immense jaws gave the creature the capability to swallow a human down with several chomps—a true man eater in every sense of the term.

Suddenly, the big head swung in his direction. Davis remained frozen in place. He wondered to himself for a second if the creature could smell him? Was he upwind or downwind of the predator? He didn't know the answers. Despite the sheer terror coursing through him for being in such close proximity to something so awe inspiringly massive, he found himself utterly entranced by the creature as he continued to gaze up at it. To be in the presence of this monstrous land predator didn't feel quite real. But as Davis got a waft of the awful stench of the creature, he was reminded of just how real these creatures in fact were.

The huge jaws suddenly parted ways. Sharp, curved teeth lined the inside of the large, cavernous space. The oversized teeth were flattened and serrated, meant for the tearing of flesh. In certain places, saliva dripped from the upper part of the jaws to the lower part.

Davis continued taking it all in. The big head lowered itself close to the ground. He saw that there were two long bony ridges that ran between the eyes down to the tip of the snout where the two huge, slitted nostrils were. There were the two immense and sharp horns that shot out from either side of its skull. They reminded him a bit of the horns of a bull. He wondered to himself if these things gored one another from time to time or even gored their potential prey to death?

Davis couldn't take his eyes off the animal despite the innate fear running through him. And for close to a minute or so of stone-cold silence, the big head towering above the forest floor did not budge, did not flinch. The creature appeared as though it were staring toward somewhere far off in the distance. And then finally with a loud rumbling snort through its nostrils, the powerful neck swung the huge head to the left, and then to the right. The creature was now staring in Davis' direction.

Davis closed his eyes. He could only hope and pray that the head didn't lower itself toward the ground where he remained crouched in hiding, rather just kept staring at its full height off into the distance. If the big head did in fact lower itself and they were exposed, they would be killed right there on the spot. There would be nothing they could do to stop the inevitable from happening. The creature would turn over the metal roof as though it were nothing, exposing all four of them, and in turn having its pick of who to feast on first. The great jaws would open wide, and the crushing teeth would close down upon each and every last one of them. Davis forced some much need air through his nostrils and remained with his eyes closed tightly. He had just slowly opened his eyes when suddenly—

The crashing sound of the huge creature's colossal feet moving rumbled through the area. The creature was once again on the move. Davis watched as the great chest cavity followed by the long and muscular tail passed right on by him. Perhaps something else had caught its attention. Perhaps it lost interest. Whatever the reason, Davis was able to breathe a momentary sigh of relief as the sound of the huge feet went stomping off into the distance.

Where're the others? he thought to himself with a chill.

Davis specifically remembered seeing perhaps a dozen or so black shapes, if not more, traveling down the building-sized creature's body as it bore down upon the right-hand side of the Bay Bridge. They had originally encountered one of these juvenile creatures, only to find that when they neared the cyclone fence that led back to the bridge, they all watched as three more of the creature's stormed the fence and entered the island. That meant that there was more than one of these massive things roaming the island. It was a terrifying reality indeed.

Davis strained with his ears to listen. He heard no sign of the huge creature. With a bit of a struggle, he managed to pull himself back underneath the cover of the large metal roof.

Davis maneuvered and slid himself back toward his family. He looked at his wife and two kids. Worry, concern, and utter terror was plastered across each of their faces.

"Is it gone?" Elena whispered, her voice quivering.

Pedro chuckled quietly to himself. "Yeah, Mom, it's gone. Kinda hard not to notice the thing as it causes a mini earthquake each time it moves."

Despite the growing severity of the situation, Pedro's comment had drawn a slight chuckle of laughter from the whole family. It had been God knows how long since any of them had even so much as cracked a smile, let alone laughed. And it felt good, damn good, even if it was only for a second or two, just a momentary reprieve from their grim reality.

Davis had felt knots forming in the pit of his stomach for quite some time now. He could only wonder what his kids were feeling and experiencing. What type of raw and scared emotions were running through their small, frightened, and confused bodies? He eyed Elena.

"Let's wait here a bit," Davis said. "Catch our breath."

Pedro tapped his dad's leg. "Dad, they're some sort of super predator. Apex predators at the top of the food chain. They would dominate and outcompete any land predator living on Earth today."

Davis smiled down at the boy. His young son never ceased to amaze him. "Right you are. Nothing in this world could match them pound for pound. Nothing. They could decimate the earth if given the chance."

Ariana suddenly reached over and punched Pedro in the gut. "Smarty pants."

The five-year-old girl had struck her brother good and Pedro sort of keeled over a bit from his seated position.

"Hey," Pedro blurted out while grabbing at his side. "She punched me."

Davis leaned forward and eyed Ariana. He whispered to her. "Ariana, we've talked about this. We don't hit, we don't punch, we don't pinch, we don't do any of those things. Understood?"

Almost immediately, Ariana started to grow flustered. She looked to her mom to come to her aid. Elena stared at her sternly.

"Oh great. Not fair," Ariana said in protest folding her arms. "You always take his side."

Davis was just about to fire something back when suddenly they heard movement from close by. Slowly, he brought his hand up to his lips, motioning for them all to be quiet. At first, they heard nothing, only the sound of the wind as it whipped the tops of the eucalyptus trees back and forth high above them. Davis strained with his ears to listen. Now it was quite evident that the wind had picked up considerably, and for a second he feared the powerful gusts might actually blow the sheet of metal right off of them.

A few more seconds of silence passed. Something was making its way down the path toward them. Davis put his hand down on the ground. He was trying to see if he felt any vibrations in the earth. Pedro, seeing this, instantly did the same thing as well. He didn't feel anything either. Like Pedro said a few minutes ago, it was hard not to notice these things. They had that going for them at least. Something that size wouldn't just sneak up on you out of the blue. When those things moved, everything in the goddamn vicinity took notice.

Davis kept his hand down on the ground for a few seconds longer. There didn't appear to be any new vibrations coming their way. Slowly, he pulled his hand back off the ground. Pedro did the same. As both of them did so, they heard what appeared to be the crunch of gravel underfoot. It sounded like someone was walking toward them. Elena reached out and hugged Ariana. Meanwhile, Pedro scooted closer toward his dad. Davis reached out and took hold of him. All they could do now together as a family was continue to wait it out and listen.

8

Matt Baker had heard every bit the commotion and then some that had just rung out from further up the hillside. Slowly, he crawled out of his hiding spot from deep within the shrubs. His heart wouldn't let up on him and was still pounding relentlessly like a set of drums. He had seen the bloody aftermath of what one of these creatures had done to their bear, and a very good-sized bear at that. What would one of these immense predators do to him? Matt shuddered just thinking of meeting his maker in such a horrific manner. He would be pulled limb from limb like a ragdoll before being eaten alive.

"Straight through the digestive track," he mumbled grimly to himself.

As Matt stood and emerged slowly and cautiously from the shrubs, he had this terrifying fear of being eaten alive, like he was bobbing stranded helpless in the ocean while sharks circled below. It was the fear of the unknown, the fear of what lay beyond that gripped him tightly now.

Try as he might, it was hard to shake the image of their precious bear though, something they had raised since it had been a cub. The manner in which it had been systemically dismantled by the creature was beyond unnerving. Matt shook his head and fought off the overwhelming urge to vomit. That wasn't right. It was unnatural, sickening, revolting, and horrifying all in one.

Matt quietly emerged from the deep vegetation and had just placed his foot down when suddenly his foot came out from underneath him. He had failed to realize that he had placed his full weight down on a thick matting of fallen eucalyptus leaves. They were slippery as hell. Matt knew he was going down. Lashing out with his hands, he tried to grab hold of the shrubs, anything.

It was too late though. In a matter of seconds, he found himself tumbling out of control down the hillside. His body, which now resembled that of a snowball, quickly got up to speed as things became a blur. As he tumbled, he had no semblance of up or down, left or right.

Somewhere in the back of his mind, behind the initial shock of losing his footing in the first place, he knew that he was shouting at the top of his lungs. And shouting at the top of his lungs at this point in the ballgame was a very bad idea. He couldn't afford to attract unwanted attention to himself.

Despite knowing this, Matt screamed at the top of his lungs as a sharp object tore and scraped his skin. He must have hit something large and jagged protruding out of the ground. Must have been a damn rock or something. Whatever it was had suddenly thrust him into a world of hot searing pain. And he was also bleeding.

He tumbled end over end. The world was now nothing more than a confusing array of blurs and shapes. As Matt rolled over one more rotation, he saw a dark blur of a shape quickly approaching from below. It was either one of these immense monsters racing up the hillside to finish him off from below or the other possibility was that it was a—

Matt collided straight into the base of one of the giant eucalyptuses that grew on this lone hillside. The impact stunned him and literally left him breathless and seeing spots in his vision.

For a moment, all Matt could do was lay motionless at the bottom of the tree, his body contorted and twisted like an accordion into a sickening array of limbs and body parts. Warily Matt opened his eyes. It took several seconds for the stars and blurry shapes to disappear from his vision. He could hardly breathe, the wind having been taken from his lungs completely by the blow from the huge base of the tree. And then in an instant it all came rushing to him. He had slipped and fallen a good way down the dirt hillside and now lay wracked in a considerable amount of pain at the base of one of the huge eucalyptus trees. He moved his fingers, arms, and legs. Everything seemed to be okay. But Matt quickly remembered that his harrowing trip down the hill had not been a quiet one. In fact, now that he thought about it, his throat burned and felt a bit raw from his screams.

Certainly, his deep guttural cries of terror hadn't gone unnoticed. Matt slowly found the courage to get himself into a crawling position before finally standing to his feet. Still wracked in a considerable amount of pain, he found his legs to be quite wobbly. As he carefully took in his surroundings, he quickly realized that it had suddenly became unnaturally quiet. There wasn't even a squawk from one of the birds high above in the canopy. The forest had fallen deathly silent.

9

For a long few seconds, Davis just sat there, the small family of four completely enshrouded in a deep and all-encompassing silence. They were uncertain as to what their next move should be.

And then just like that they heard noise in the form of movement. It appeared to be coming their way.

Davis took a deep breath and clenched his fists. He sure as hell wished that he had secured some type of weapon, a hammer, gardening tool, anything at all. Anything was better than nothing. Clenching his fists into two tight balls of potential energy, he realized that those two fists of his were all they had right now.

As the noise drew closer and closer, Davis knew with certainty that it was indeed not one of the creatures. Things would be shaking and vibrating within the small confines of their makeshift shelter if it indeed was one of the gargantuan carnivores. But nonetheless there was noise quietly making its way toward them. His fists remained bunched and tightened, ready to defend his family to the death if it called for it.

For a moment he looked down at his swollen and scarred knuckles, knuckles that had seen one too many fights in his teenage years and even into his early twenties.

Barroom brawls, nightclubs, metal concerts, and even into his collegiate football playing days. He had fought, and he had fought way too often. It was also those same very hands that had led him to play college football at the running back position. They were strong and powerful hands, and he knew it. And throughout his life they had always aided him whenever the moment or situation called for it. Right now, on this island of horrors was most definitely one of those moments.

Davis' senses tightened on him, becoming razor sharp. He heard what appeared to be shoes atop the gravel from the path. The sound of gravel crunching underfoot continued for a while longer before finally coming to a complete stop.

All four of them waited and listened as the sound once again picked back up. The noise drew even closer. And then it came to a complete stop. Whatever it was appeared to be just outside their hiding spot. Davis eyed Elena for a brief glance.

Davis thought he noticed the faintest trace of deodorant or cheap aftershave in the air. It had that same bad smell and reminded him of the godawful aftershave his grandfather used to wear.

A few more tense and uncomfortable seconds passed by before suddenly without warning, their makeshift shelter was pulled back violently. With a heavy thud the metal roof toppled to the ground.

The muscles in Davis' body twinged with anticipation, and just as he had done time and time again back in his collegiate football playing days, he sprung to life. Surging with adrenaline, his powerful leg muscles thrust his body upward, forcing himself to his feet. He was just about ready to pounce on whomever or whatever had torn their makeshift roof off when suddenly he found himself staring down the barrel of a shotgun.

"I knew I shoulda done away with you folk back there when I had the chance," the man said pointing the barrel of the shotgun straight at Davis. "I asked nice before but I'm afraid I can't be nice this time round. Can't trust folk these days ya know."

Davis went to take a step forward but immediately felt the barrel of the shotgun jammed straight into his chest. He felt the heavy weapon against him now.

"I wouldn't if I were you, son," the man said, forcing Davis back down to the ground and into a seated position. "I just wouldn't."

Davis had a seat next to his family, and together the four sat completely helpless and at the mercy of this individual. Davis looked up at the overwhelmingly fat bearded man. This was the same asshole that they'd encountered just a short while ago who'd been hanging his body out the open window of the second level of the building who had refused to help them. The man had long disheveled shoulder length black hair, hairy arms to go along with a hairy neck, and a beard that grew a good way down from the man's saggy and round bottom of his chin. The barrel of the shotgun remained pointed squarely at Davis the entire time.

Davis had just begun sizing the man up and working out a potential course of action when out of nowhere he noticed the faintest sensation. The ground beneath them tremored ever so slightly. Without taking his eyes off the man, he reached with his right hand and laid his palm down flat on the ground.

Meanwhile, Davis' movement hadn't gone unnoticed. The fat man shook his head back and forth while cocking the shotgun. "I told you, boy, not to move. What is it with you youngin's and not followin' the rules these days?"

Leveling the barrel in the direction of Davis' head, suddenly it felt like a small earthquake had appeared out of nowhere. Davis turned just in time to witness an immense shape emerge, momentarily blotting out the sun. Next, he saw a set of immense jaws housing teeth bigger than bananas open impossibly wide. With it came an overwhelming wave of stench. The huge jaws crashed down over the fat man and instantly swept him up and off the ground as if he weighed but a mere few pounds.

Davis heard the gun go off from somewhere deep within the monster's jaws as the man was lifted higher and into the air. And then his eyes went wide as he saw the shotgun fall from the great beast's mouth. It made a loud clattering sound as it hit the ground hard.

Meanwhile from high above, legs protruded out and were pinned in place by the massive teeth. Davis watched as the big head whipped itself back and forth violently, the legs of the man being thrown from side to side as if he were on a rollercoaster.

Davis realized in that moment that this was his chance. He scrambled forward and raced out to retrieve the shotgun. Legs as big as tree trunks stood in his way as the creature threw its enormous bulk around in an attempt to consume the large man whole. As Davis carefully navigated his way around the massive feet and limbs of the beast, he could still hear the fat man struggling from deep within the huge set of cavernous jaws. He ultimately knew that close to twenty feet above the ground, in a set of monstrous jaws that must have been damn near six feet in length, it was essentially a suicide mission with one outcome and one outcome only. Death.

Davis was yards away from the shotgun when the giant creature threw its enormous bulk around once more and brought one of its huge feet crashing down atop the weapon. Davis felt his eyes go wide on him with the sudden realization that the full weight of the creature had smashed the gun flat to the ground. With the huge foot now resting heavily on the shotgun and the other giant hind limb standing in his way like a big tree, Davis quickly changed his course of action.

He flung himself around. The creature meanwhile was still preoccupied with its rather large meal. This was their chance to officially get themselves out of the area. Davis had no way of knowing how long the meal would curb the great beast's appetite.

Davis rushed forward, running underneath the creature's immense spiked tail. As he did so he was greeted with an up close and personal view of just how truly huge these things in fact were. Emerging out from underneath the cover of the long tail, he was able to get a good glimpse of the beast as he stared up at it. Ragged flesh hung in shredded strands from the lower jaws.

When the huge creature once again swung its giant body along with its huge tail through the air, that was all the wakeup call that Davis needed. He sprinted back to his family. Davis had just reached down to lift both Pedro and Ariana from the ground when suddenly from behind them an enormous cracking and crunching sound rang out. This was followed by several wet, gurgled screams from inside the immense set of jaws. One last final scream rang out before being cut off and replaced with the sound of bones crunching and grinding.

Davis bent down and picked up Pedro off the ground. He motioned for Elena to get Ariana. She did the same, lifting their young daughter up and into her arms. Now both parents held both kids tight to their chests.

Davis looked back to Elena. "Need to get to somewhere safe, more protected and secure than this."

But as Davis said those very words to his wife, seeing all that they had already witnessed and experienced, he wondered if such a safe and secure place actually existed. Sure, there were homes on the island, but given the nature of the pandemic, the global financial recession, coupled lastly with the horrendous fires, meant that people had boarded up their homes and weren't willing to help one another out. It was now a dog-eat-dog world, very much survival of the fittest in every sense of the word. Tough times called for tough measures and they were now seeing the lasting effects of those measures right this very minute.

Elena edged just ahead of her husband, scanning back and forth frantically for anywhere where it would appear as though they could take up refuge. The entire time they had been scrambling their way up a rather steep hillside. Finally, the brute of a hill flattened out a bit and gave way to a small road. They crossed the road and immediately entered into another thick forested area on the island. The dense grove of trees transitioned into a dry steep sloping part of the island that fell downward. Down below and on their right side, Davis could see the blue waters of the San Francisco Bay. He knew just where they were on the island. It was the part of Yerba Buena that was visible from the Bay Bridge when traffic was heading out of the city. He had seen this dry steep part of the island many times before when leaving San Francisco but had never actually traversed it.

On their righthand side the island fell off at a steep decline to the cold water of the San Francisco Bay about a hundred feet or so below. With Pedro secured tightly in his arms, both Davis and Elena held their respective lines as they traversed across the island. Davis didn't want them getting any closer to the steep drop off that existed to their right. The terrain sloped downward at a sharp angle before giving way to what could best be described as dirt cliffs. It almost felt as though this part of the island was working with gravity to pull everything within close range to the drop off at the edge.

Davis continued to hold his course down the hillside, not allowing them to get any closer toward the drop off. They moved across hard and compacted earth. The long grass that did grow in this part of the island was very dry.

"Careful," Davis shouted.

He knew that the hard and compacted ground coupled with the dry wispy grass made ideal conditions for slipping. To their left, tall stands of eucalyptus trees grew rather spaced out from one another.

And then from somewhere back near the top of the hillside, they heard a chilling rumbling sound cut through the air. It reminded Davis of hearing lions wailing and roaring on the Serengeti in Africa. But beyond that it also meant one thing—the creature had officially consumed the man. The meal was over. Would it be looking for its next quick meal, but more importantly when? Davis didn't know. They kept moving carefully across the island.

***

Having just fed twice in a relatively short period of time, consuming hundreds of pounds of fresh raw meat, the young carnivore found its appetite momentarily curbed. Looking around, the big head turned in the direction of the two-story white building. It eyed the building for a moment. And then with several loud crashing steps, it moved forward in that direction.

Meanwhile, the huge creature that had just fed on the man had not gone unnoticed. From behind a thick wall of eucalyptus trees, three equally enormous heads peeked their way out, their massive forms momentarily hidden behind the bases of the trees. Not more than fifty yards away from where the three hyper carnivores stood, they patiently eyed one of their own. Moving slowly, they knew the creature that they were eyeing had just fed. Its movements had slowed down considerably. It had fed twice and while its belly was momentarily content and satisfied, there were others that hadn't been so fortunate, needed to feel the sensation of raw meat going down their throats and into their enormous chest cavities. Their bloodlust was insatiable at this point.

One of the enormous creatures stepped out and into the open. With a mouth full of wet glistening teeth, the jaws of the huge beast parted ways as it eyed its sibling. Suddenly another creature emerged from behind the row of trees, followed lastly by one more. Now the three immense predators stood there, their huge heads towering above the ground, their stomachs rumbling with hunger as they continued to eye their potential prey.

Meanwhile, from a short distance away, the original creature that had killed and eaten the fat man not more than thirty minutes ago continued moving close to the white building, unaware that it was being watched, unaware that it had potentially been marked for death. The huge creature stopped for a moment. The big head swung up and eyed in the direction of the open window. It had no clue what to make of the large building or the open window for that matter. It just stared for a while longer before finally continuing on its way. It saw an area that was littered with leaves. It looked soft, just the perfect place to bed down for a while and rest after its big meal.

As the fifty-foot-long animal continued making its way toward the soft bedding where it planned on lying down for a bit, suddenly there was an enormous explosion from somewhere close by. The creature threw its mass around, the huge tail smashing into part of the building as it scrambled to gain semblance of what was happening.

The creature turned just in time to see three enormous shapes barreling toward it. The ground rumbled and shook as what had to be close to sixty thousand pounds in combined weight moved toward it like a tidal wave about to make landfall. With each creature moving at top speed, they blared gaping roars. The scene itself resembled something ripped straight from the time of the dinosaurs. This was survival of the fittest at its finest, an adage known since the dawn of time.

Completely surprised and caught off guard, the solitary predator had little time to do anything except mount its own attack. Rushing out in great huge strides to greet the three oncoming attackers, the beast set its sights firmly on the creature in the middle. Letting loose a terrifying cry from within its great jaws, it bounded forward.

With claws forward facing and ready to inflict maximum damage, the lone creature prepared to do battle. The solitary creature opened its jaws as wide as it could and had just sunk its teeth into the side of the creature when suddenly it was thrust into its own world of fiery explosive pain. The two remaining predators had not hesitated to bite down onto the thick leathery sides of its body. One bit down with crushing force into the muscularly built tail of the lone creature while another sunk blood-thirsty teeth into the powerful neck muscles.

While the solitary creature managed to bite down and into the neck of the creature in the middle, quickly the lone creature felt itself being overpowered. It was simply no match for the two creatures that had bit down and attached themselves to both sides of its body now.

The two predators were literally pulling the animal down to the ground now. The small pack of predators worked in coordinated efforts to take their prey down.

Outmanned and overpowered, the creature was quickly losing this battle. Visibly bleeding and weakened from blood loss, the crushing jaws released their grip around the other animal's neck. This momentary window gave the original creature in the middle of the pack all the opportunity it needed. With a sharp tug, it pulled its neck free from the great jaws of the solitary predator. Now it was truly three against one as the lone predator roared and shot forward. The giant animals fought as huge limbs collided, powerful tails slammed into one another, sharp oversized claws dug in and tore away at flesh wherever they could, and jaws bigger than a man blared menacingly to one another.

One of the predators on the far left side wasted no time as it lunged and bit down upon the neck of the solitary creature. Now this pack of three was literally seconds away from toppling their wounded and injured prey to the ground. The mouths and teeth gripped and sunk down into the flesh and muscle of the screaming animal and simply would not let go. And just in the same manner as a Nile crocodile bites onto a crossing wildebeest at the river's edge only to drag it down into the murky waters for an untimely death, so too did the three creatures. Biting down with untold force, the three predators finally succeeded in toppling their prey to the ground.

There was an enormous explosion of sound as the twenty-thousand-pound predator collapsed onto its side. Huge plumes of dirt and debris were sent up into the air on account of the impact.

When the fallen predator appeared as though it might actually right itself and stand back up, one of the other creatures countered by placing an enormous, manhole-sized foot atop the animal, pinning the fallen predator to the ground under its weight and sharp toe claws. Wasting no time, it lowered its neck, opened its huge jaws, and sunk its teeth into the side of the injured creature.

There was an immense scream that seemed to harken back to another world as teeth punctured through hide, meat, and even bone. Another one of the massive creatures came over to the side of the great fallen beast, placed its own giant clawed foot down atop the side of the huge stomach, and with a quick downward motion, dragged and raked its clawed feet over the hide. Within seconds, deep and bleeding gouge marks could be seen in the creature's flesh.

The fallen behemoth lay helpless in a growing pool of its own blood as it let loose a cavernous cry while another one of the creatures began to pull and rake out some of its ribs. It wasn't long before several of the creature's ribs had been pulled out through the skin and now lay open and exposed by the monster working diligently to end its life.

With several of its ribs laying partially exposed, the creature on the ground began thrashing about wildly, limbs, legs, and tail smashing and thumping into the ground relentlessly. It wouldn't be long now.

More biting, clawing, and gouging ensued. All of this culminated in one final death scream from the once mighty land predator. The scream which blasted out over the landscape suddenly cut off abruptly. The short lived yet violent struggle had taken the life of this gigantic beast. The huge animal lay there, completely still and motionless, a giant pool of warm, crimson blood slowly starting to seep and spread beneath its body. It lay there, the huge gaping mouth permanently open and contorted into one last harrowing cry. What had once been a fifty-foot-long nightmarish creature was quickly being reduced to a bloodied, torn, and mangled carcass. With deep gouge marks and ribs exposed, the creature now lay a shell of its former self, a small mountain of mangled flesh as blood continued to gush from the open wounds.

Meanwhile the three attackers now stood towering over their kill. Hungry mouths needed to feed, and an opportunity was an opportunity. In unison, all three huge-cavernous jaws opened together as one. Low bellowing, rumbling sounds emanated from the jaws as ropes of saliva dripped from the top rows of teeth. And then, like a pack of oversized hungry wolves, the three predators tore into their fresh kill.

10

Davis Brown and his family had heard every bit of the carnage from behind them and then some. In some faint yet distant part of his memory, one that still remembered familiar activities such as sitting down and watching tv, the terrifying noise had sounded a bit like he was watching a documentary on lions or some other type of big predator on Discovery Channel or NatGeo. The ungodly savage moaning cries sounded just like that, with big gaping roars that seemingly stretched on and on forever. And then there had been the screaming, the haunting, chilling sounds of an injured animal kicking and scrambling for its very existence. He remembered the deep moaning howl of a roar that cut off abruptly.

The taking of a life, he thought to himself grimly.

Surely the abrupt way in which that cry had cut off out of nowhere certainly signified death itself. What was even worse than the actual sounds of death itself was the stark reality that his two young kids had also heard every bit of the fighting struggle as well. There was no way to sugarcoat things, no way to hide it; their kids were now both seeing, hearing, and experiencing in real time the true nightmare that they now found themselves thrust into.

Traversing down the hard dirt that made up the hillside, a thick forest of trees grew just to their left. And on their right side, the island still dropped off abruptly to the cold waters of the bay below.

"Be careful," Davis called out to Elena who was in front of him.

"I got it," she yelled back to him, still holding Ariana firmly in her arms as she ran. "We're okay."

The trees that dotted this part of the island and which had been for the most part in the foreground on their downward descent, suddenly started to become more prominent. Before Davis or Elena could do anything more about it, they found themselves dodging trees left and right. The forest had once again come back into play.

For a short while they navigated and weaved their way through these thick passages of trees before finally emerging once again out into the open. Immediately, bright light streamed down upon them, and Davis quickly realized that the thick smokey air must have momentarily cleared just enough to allow for the sun to peak its head through. The air quality had also improved considerably. It felt good to see the sun again, if only for a short window of time.

"Mommy, look," Ariana shouted from up ahead while pointing with her tiny fingers.

Together, the family turned in unison. What they saw rocked them to the core. The momentary opening in the trees gave them a clear and unobstructed view back to the Bay Bridge.

"Oh my God," Elena blurted out while covering her mouth. "What on Earth?"

By now they had all come to a panting stop to have a look back to the bridge, and to take in the pure devastation that had been inflicted upon it.

Davis knew that what they were witnessing and taking in would be there. It was almost as if in some strange, detached part of his brain he didn't want to fully come to terms with it though. It was difficult to take in the horrific site that had taken place a short while ago.

A good hundred or so feet of bridge had been ripped and torn away as though it had never even existed. Now Davis and his family could see the concrete with steel reinforced rebar sticking out from the part of the bridge that had been torn away and collapsed.

It felt highly inappropriate to call the animal that had risen from the water and torn part of the bridge away like it was nothing an *animal*. Davis didn't know what to call the creature that had inflicted massive devastation on the bridge with several swipes from its enormous-clawed limbs. It was an aberration that for all, intents and purposes, had crawled and climbed its way out of the depths of hell. In a strange yet detached part of his brain, Davis couldn't quite shake the thought that perhaps the beast had come straight from the center of the Earth, from a place of fire and magma, from a completely different world from that up on the surface. Still though, it was a far-fetched theory and too much for him to take in at this point in time.

Davis felt sick to his stomach to see nothing but open air in place of what had to be a good hundred feet or so of where part of the Bay Bridge used to be. It had all crumbled and fallen into the water below when the monstrous creature had literally shaken the earth to its core by its arrival in the San Francisco Bay.

Davis set Pedro down on the ground. The eight-year-old boy pressed forward several feet toward the edge of the hillside where things dropped straight down to the water below. Davis reached out and grabbed his son. And together father and son moved forward, stopping about a dozen feet or so from where the cliff dropped straight down to the water below.

"Careful," Elena cried out from behind them, still holding Ariana in her arms.

Now Davis and Pedro looked out and gazed at the water below the bridge where possibly hundreds of cars with people trapped inside them had more than likely plunged to their untimely deaths. The water beneath that part of the bridge was eerily calm, as though it had just swallowed up a great big secret. Davis shuddered to himself thinking about all those people trapped helplessly in their cars drowning to death. The water below the bridge had also erased all evidence of the collapsed section of the bridge as well. Davis looked back up one last time toward where the section of the bridge had been torn away and then back down to the cold water below. It was close to a two-hundred foot drop. He felt a chill with the grim reality of just how large the number of deaths possibly was.

And then his eyes locked in on the San Francisco skyline for a moment just on the other side of the bay. The scene itself looked like something out of a Hollywood blockbuster movie. The vast majority of the city lay enshrouded behind a dark covering of smoke and clouds. Only the tops of several of the taller buildings could be seen peeking their heads above the smoke and cloud cover. The immense Sales Force Tower was the most visible building of them all. Davis eyed that towering monstrosity of a building for a moment longer before returning his view back to the city. For the most part, the entire city lay behind a thick veil of fog.

Fire, plague, protests, looming financial apocalypse, he thought to himself grimly. *The end of days.*

For a moment, Davis thought back to his brief discussion with his good friend Pedro from Lisbon, Portugal. The two had gone to graduate school together in San Francisco and Davis had in fact named his son in honor of his great friend. But now as he stood there next to his son and took in the sight of part of the Bay Bridge that had broken off and the post-apocalyptic feel that the city had suddenly taken on, maybe it really was the end of days as his good friend had spoken of recently. Could it actually be true?

All of a sudden, Davis felt tapping on his thigh. His head swung downward. Pedro looked up at him, fighting back and wiping away at the tears.

"Dad, I wanna go home," Pedro said sniffling.

In that moment Davis not only felt the enormity of the situation hit him square on, but he literally felt his heart sink. For the first time today since exiting their car, Pedro had reminded him that while he may have been mature for his age and more often than not seemed older than he actually was, that he was simply an eight-year-old boy that missed his home. He was a young kid that desperately wanted to get back to the safety of home. And who could blame him? Davis felt exactly the same way as well.

Still, with that overwhelming sinking feeling deep within his chest, Davis kneeled down to Pedro's level.

"I wanna go home too," Davis said, touching Pedro

on the kneecap. "We will. I promise we will soon."

Father and son embraced for a quick hug. Davis didn't want to let go. Fighting back tears of his own, he had to do everything in his power to get his family safely off this hellhole of an island. This was his sole mission on this earth now. Tilting his head to the side, he could see that Ariana had come in for a hug as well and had now latched onto his right shoulder. Lastly, Elena joined in to complete the warm and inviting family embrace. And for the briefest of moments, they all held tight to one another.

"Dad, these things are ginormous, as big as the largest of any of monstrous predatory dinosaurs from the past. If not bigger. How do we beat them?"

Davis took a moment as he was still trying to wrap his head around the building-sized creature that had taken out part of the bridge. He wiped at his nose for a second before attempting to respond to Pedro's question. "Son, it's not a matter of defeating these things, but rather evading and steering clear of them. We need to choose stealth over brawns."

"What's that mean?" Ariana asked in a silly voice.

Elena took the question. "It just means, sweetie, that we can't fight these things, rather we just need to do our best to steer clear of them, stay out of their way. We want nothing to do with them and want to avoid them completely."

Davis watched as Pedro's face suddenly molded into that of a smile, not a smile that signified happiness, but rather one that signified the gears upstairs in the brain were busy at work churning.

Davis nodded and smiled to his son.

"Yeah," Pedro replied, nodding his head, seeming to

reaffirm what his dad had just said. "I like that idea, Dad. I like it a lot. You don't have to be the fastest out there, just faster than those around you. Right, Dad?"

Davis rubbed Pedro's head playfully for a moment, father and son sharing another quick yet fleeting embrace.

"Oh sure," Ariana suddenly blurted out. "Mr. smarty pants is a poopy head."

Davis reached around and gave Ariana a big hug as well. "You're both smart. End of story. You're brother's a few years older than you. That's all. By the time you're his age, I'm sure you'll be way smarter than he is."

Ariana smiled and stuck her tongue out in Pedro's direction. Pedro had just stuck his tongue out at his sister when out of nowhere an enormous gaping roar filled the air. The chilling, harrowing cry appeared to have come from somewhere above them.

Davis wasted no time as he helped his family to their feet. And just like that they were once again on the move, traversing safely down one side of the island. Pedro and Ariana ran at both he and Elena's sides. Davis grabbed Ariana's hand and Elena took hold of Pedro's.

As they continued descending further and further toward the bottom of the island, a second unearthly cry rang out. They now knew with certainty that there appeared to be more than one of these things pursuing them. It was hard to tell if they had been officially spotted or not, but the only thing they could do was to keep up their speed and navigate their toward the bottom of the island now.

"Gotta keep movin'," Davis reiterated.

Another deep moaning cry from somewhere behind them pushed them all to up their speed. Something most definitely was heading their way. At this point though, Davis was too busy helping them all successfully navigate their way down to have a look back. All he could do now was maintain his grip with his right hand on Ariana's.

Pushing his family in the direction of left, they exited the edge of the island and once again began moving more inland toward the middle of the island. With this new course of direction meant-

Trees. Lots of them. Davis and his family quickly found themselves navigating through another thick track of forest, tall-towering eucalyptus mixed with French broom at ground level. The terrain continued to fall downward at a sharp angle. Davis had a pretty good idea of just where they were heading. When they finally got an opening, a break in the trees just up ahead, they could see what Davis had hoped for all along. A large dock which ran for hundreds of feet in both directions lay at the bottom of the island. That's just where they were headed.

***

The two massive heads lined with sharp serrated teeth the size of bananas suddenly pushed through the tree line at the very top of the hillside. But instead of proceeding down the hill, they thundered off horizontally, plowing and snaking their way through the dense stands of eucalyptus. Towering above the ground, their hulking forms absolutely dominated the landscape. Two huge eyes sunk deep into their skulls guided them forward. Their long and muscular tails snaked and weaved their way around the trees, providing the counter-balance needed to support their enormous weight.

They brought their huge bodies to a stop near the

base of a large eucalyptus tree. Both creatures just stood there for a moment. One of the animals suddenly shifted its weight, and in doing so brushed up against one of the trees. The result was a loud cracking sound as the wood split and broke in that particular part of the tree. The huge head raised high up and surveyed the forest. When no further sounds of life came, both creatures began moving through the forest once again toward an open area of light where there appeared to be a break in the trees. They pushed on through the trees toward the source of the light.

11

Matt Baker had been crouched in hiding the entire time behind the wheel of an old and dilapidated, rusted out car. He had partially seen what had just transpired a short while ago, but mostly he had heard the pack of three predators as they converged and took down one of their own. Already, he vowed that the audible sounds he had just bore witness to, would live with him for as long as he was still drawing breath on this Earth. Even if he tried, he didn't think he'd ever be able to forget the sounds of carnage and slaughter that he heard a short while ago. It had sounded like lions on the Serengeti of Africa feasting and pulling a carcass apart, times ten. There had been deep rumblings from their chests, primal screams that seemed to be from eons ago, and a general sense that nothing quite like them had ever roamed this planet before.

Taking all this into consideration, Matt was literally scared the fuck out of his mind, unsure as to what his next move should be. He felt glued to hiding just behind the hood of the car, his muscles seeming as though they had gone into temporary paralysis and shut down on him.

Matt forced himself to breathe, the air shuddering in and out of his chest as uncomfortably as if he were scuba diving. He couldn't quite shake the sound of their huge monstrous bodies colliding into one another, tails slamming hard against thick walls of muscle, the gouging of flesh, the breaking of bones, the taking of a life.

Matt could still hear the sound of several of the creatures as they latched viciously onto their prey and began tearing and ripping. And then he remembered that final brutal moment where all three giant predators gripped onto their prey just seconds before toppling it to the ground. The impact of all that tonnage hitting the ground was like a small bomb going off as it sent both dust and debris up into the air in one great big plume.

Matt looked up momentarily toward the sky. He could still see particles of dust and dirt floating down toward the earth like tiny snowflakes. He brought his gaze back down to ground level and adjusted his positioning. His legs were starting to cramp up on him a bit. He wasn't certain how long he had in fact been crouched in hiding behind the car like this. All he knew with certainty was that his legs felt as though they were literally about to give out any second.

He had just moved himself forward ever so slightly when he heard the all too familiar sound of tearing and chewing. Matt froze. He could hear deep resonating breaths as they shuddered in and out of huge chest cavities. It honestly reminded him of being up close and personal to huge walruses when he was younger, watching and experiencing the terrifying vocalizations they made as the air rumbled in and out of their massive blubbery bodies. These animals had that same type of deep resonating power to it.

He listened intently to the breathing and tearing for a few moments longer. It gave him the chills just thinking of such horrific creatures. But worst of all was the fact that the noise reminded him as to what was still out there, still roaming and stalking this island. They had all been thrust violently against their will into the food chain, and that positioning on the food chain was not where any human being would want to find themselves.

Matt heard more chewing followed by the sickening sound of the breaking and cracking of bones. And then all of a sudden he heard what appeared to be several of the creatures as they went thundering off into the brush. By the sound of it, he suspected they were headed back toward the edge of the island where a dense forest of eucalyptus trees grew. But it was hard to tell, hard to make sense of anything at this point.

Now, as Matt continued to listen to the lone creature feeding, he had forgotten all about the ache and strain in his legs. He listened for a few seconds longer. The sounds of chewing and ribs being broken and torn from the carcass told him it was probably okay to move forward. So that's just what he did. Getting down on his hands and knees, Matt Baker began to crawl through the dirt toward the front of the vehicle. As he drew closer to the hood of the car, he paused right where he was.

He listened and waited. Just on the other side of the car, possibly fifty feet or so away, one of the creatures was feeding, crunching bones, tearing huge chunks of flesh from the carcass. Matt's heart pounded. It was terrifying yet also at the same time exhilarating to be in such close proximity to such a breathtakingly true maneater.

Matt waited for another minute or so before finding the courage to move himself forward once again. With the front bumper on the left side of his body, he scooted himself forward and had a look out around the front of the car. He just needed to take a quick peek of what was going on.

Matt caught a glimpse of the massively constructed tail of the creature lifted high and into the air, swishing gently back and forth as the huge predator continued to feed. Next, he saw the two big hind legs, each as wide around as a good-sized tree. The massive head of the thing was buried into the exposed chest cavity of the other one of their kind. It was quite the chilling sight as the predator continued to rip and tear, stripping flesh from bone in great ragged chunks. The sickening slurping sound of entrails flopping to the ground could also be heard from time to time.

The giant predator suddenly pulled back, the huge head lifting high into the air as it turned to the side. From where Matt was positioned, he saw ragged chunks of flesh hanging from the lower jaw of the beast. The front tip of the massive snout was stained and darkened with crimson colored blood. The head swung further to the right. The enormous baseball-sized eye twitched, almost as if it had locked in on something. For a moment, Matt wondered what type of vision these things possessed. The big head swung further in his direction. Quickly, Matt pulled himself down behind the hood of the car.

Tucking himself out of view, he wondered if he had he been spotted? His heart was absolutely beating at a million miles per hour now. He started to panic. He closed his eyes for a moment and tried to control his breathing, tried to get a grip on things. But it was almost impossible. From an uncomfortably close distance away, an animal that possessed awe inspiring dimensions stood feeding. It was hard for him to breathe right about now as his mind struggled to take in the true size of the creature.

The creature took several steps forward. An awful wave of stench seemed to accompany it wherever it went. Matt remained frozen. The animal brought itself to a stop, the huge head towering above the ground as it surveyed the landscape from side to side. Matt could hear the monstrous thing breathing now as air shuddered in and out of the enormous chest cavity. The air moving in and out of the chest was a terrifying thing to witness and experience from such a close proximity.

And then he once again heard the animal's big feet moving it forward.

Oh my God, he thought to himself with the realization that the animal appeared to be moving in his direction.

Giant steps continued coming toward him.

And then suddenly an enormous shadow cast itself over the car. Matt stopped breathing altogether. Out of the corner of his left eye he was just barely able to see an enormous leg capped off by a huge foot. Sharp black oversized curved claws adorned the huge foot. Twitching up with his eye, he saw the enormous chest cavity of the animal as it breathed in and out. The mass of the chest seemed to be as wide around as that of an elephant, if not more. It was tough to comprehend just how large and imposing these animals were.

The creature remained poised in silence, the big head towering above the ground, the two eyes ever present and watchful. It was the dead silence of the situation that really got to Matt. Any noise or sound on his part and his cover would be blown, his location exposed. All he could do was just sit and wait now; see how this whole thing was going to play out.

When a great heaving breath shuddered in and out of the huge chest cavity, Matt Baker found the courage necessary to push his view past the massive chest and toward the thick neck and huge head.

The creature had its huge jaws parted just enough to see partially into the gaping mouth. He saw wet, sharp, banana-sized teeth. Teeth meant to inflict a devastating bite into their prey. Teeth meant to end life. There was no way to sugarcoat it.

Beyond the innate fear coursing through his body, Matt still had the strange wherewithal about him to think about the possibility of a species like this taking over the entire planet. It most likely wouldn't happen overnight, but in time he could see such a horrific concept becoming reality. Huge with no natural enemies. Nothing would be able to stop these things.

He watched as the big head suddenly swung to the left. The creature stared in the opposite direction from where Matt remained crouched in hiding.

Reaching out with his right hand, he picked up a small rock. He brought his hand back just enough to give the rock a good toss. The rock sailed through the air a good ways before finally hitting something with a distinct *clang*.

A deep bellowing snort followed almost immediately as the big head swung in the direction of the sound. And then with large and commanding steps, the giant predator went crashing off in the direction of the noise. Matt watched as the huge chest cavity and long powerful tail passed by him until finally disappearing out of view.

For a moment he just sat there, resting his head back against the side of the car. He felt absolutely breathless as his brain struggled to come back online. It was an innate fear of how he could possibly meet his own demise that held him pinned tightly to the car. It was the idea of being eaten alive, of being swept off the ground, crushed in place by the huge teeth, and forced into the gaping maw and down the throat that held his full attention now.

To be killed, eaten, and digested only to come out the other end, he thought grimly to himself.

For now, he realized that he was at least safe for the time being. And with that, Matt Baker lay his head back against the side of the car and closed his eyes.

12

The helicopter rose higher and higher into the sky until finally breaking free of the thick smoke and cloud cover. It seemed like the entire city of San Francisco, and surrounding Bay Area for that matter, was permanently engulfed in a thick and all-encompassing smoke due to the fires burning up north. The chopper finally pulled itself free from the last of the smoke and got its first clear and unobstructed view of the San Francisco-Oakland Bay Bridge and surrounding Yerba Buena Island.

"Jesus Christ," the pilot remarked as he pulled the helicopter higher into the sky.

They were going to circle back around, get a better view. It was the KTVU Channel 2 news helicopter, and they were here to film, document, and keep citizens abreast of the brewing situation.

The pilot looked down at the mess through his dark aviator sunglasses. He eyed the part of the bridge that had broken off, been torn away. His mind reeled as he struggled to take in the enormity of everything. It was honestly the most surreal sight that any of them had ever seen before, the part of the bridge being torn away like that and all. Looking down at the water below, he realized the possibility of those that had been trapped in their cars when this portion of the bridge had collapsed, meant that finding survivors at this point seemed unlikely. The death toll would be in the hundreds. It was almost inconceivable.

The chopper began circling the island. Cold air rushed in from the open hatch as they began to film and document things. To the pilot it honestly felt like they had all been thrust into the very depths of hell itself. Even before they had taken to the air, they were already well aware of the wild and crazy claims that a creature as big as a building had suddenly emerged from the bay itself and bore down upon the helpless Bay Bridge. Already, there had been postings on social media documenting the arrival of the monstrous creature, some still photos while others managed to capture the creature's wrath of devastation as it tore part of the bridge away, sending hundreds of cars to their watery graves.

They remained focused on their mission though. That mission objective was to broadcast live footage from high in the sky to television, just what was going on down below. They all had a job to do, no matter how grim or morbid the reality of the growing situation may have been. And that's just what they were doing right this very minute.

The pilot took the helicopter out in a big arching circle now. Down below he eyed the steep forested slopes of Yerba Buena Island. As they drew closer to one of the thick forested slopes, the pilot saw a momentary break in the eucalyptus trees. And as he looked closer, he could see people down below. He lowered his glasses for a moment. The figures suddenly came out into the open on a large green grassy field.

From the height at which they were circling the island, the people appeared as tiny dots, but they were people nonetheless. And they were running. As he continued to take it all in from high in the sky, he realized there were far more running dots down there than he had initially expected. Where were they running to? He honestly had no clue, just that it appeared as though they were headed down the hill toward the bottom of the island where things transitioned to a large dock. He stared for a while longer out the side window.

Now he had the helicopter hovering directly over another forested sloping part of the island. The pilot continued to look down. He could see the gaps and breaks in between the trees. A few more seconds of staring and he saw more shapes weaving their way through the trees.

More people. What the fuck?

What in the bloody hell was going on down there? He scratched his head as he continued to stare.

The voice of someone shouting over the rotor wash broke him from his thoughts. The voice cut in from behind him. It was the Channel 2 KTVU News crew. They were filming and doing their thing. As KTVU continued to capture and document footage from the open hatch of the chopper, the helicopter pilot's attention once again shifted back to the tops of the trees below. He watched for a few seconds longer before all visual signs of people finally faded off. Now there was nothing but the tops of the eucalyptus towering a hundred feet or so above ground blowing back and forth in the wind.

The pilot was just about to shift his attention back to the Bay Bridge when suddenly he caught sight of something. Moving and snaking its way through the trees, he got a visual of a rather large blur of a shape. At first, he thought nothing of it; thought perhaps his eyes were deceiving him. It had already been an incredibly long work shift and there was still so much more to go. The pilot took his glasses off and clipped them onto the collar of his shirt. Now he focused his sole attention back down below once again.

He saw nothing, only the tops of the trees. Whatever it was had moved on or simply disappeared. And then just like that there was a quick flash of something moving swiftly through the trees. He saw what looked to be a big body followed by a long and powerful tail navigating its way through the trees, almost as if it was pursuing something. He froze in his seat, the chopper still hovering in place several hundred feet above the island.

Forcing himself to remain calm and get a grip on things, he tried to locate the large shape that he had just seen moving through the trees. Scanning the top of the canopy turned up nothing though. Where the hell had it gone? All he knew was that whatever he had just seen appeared to have some good size to it when compared to the size of the tiny human dots.

The pilot took one more look out his window to see if he could spot anything. Nothing. But he did notice one thing. Judging by how hard the tops of the eucalyptus trees were rocking back and forth, he could see that the wind had finally started to pick back up. It was really blowing quite hard now.

"Bout damn time," he muttered to himself, hoping that the wind would finally clear the city of this god-awful smoke once and for all.

He took the helicopter out and away from the island in a wide turn now. He knew what he had seen. Something had been moving through the trees in pursuit of all those people. The only question that remained on his mind was just what in the hell could it have been?

13

"Daddy, how much further?" Ariana cried out from Elena's arms.

Davis brought his family to a much-needed stop. Both Elena and he had once again taken to carrying the kids. Consequently, they were quite winded. They just needed to catch their breaths for a moment. They had navigated and made their way down the hillside more than three quarters of the way now. They were still surrounded on all sides by tall trees but it wouldn't be much further until they reached a long cement pier which ran for a considerable length in both directions at the very bottom of the island.

As Davis breathed in a big lungful of air though, he knew full well that they weren't alone. There were others following in the same direction, navigating through the same stretch of forest that they had just traversed through. They could hear them now as the forest around them was abuzz with noise.

Davis knew that his family was utterly exhausted and in desperate need of a break. But they weren't going to get one. As the sounds of people quickly moving toward them reached him, Davis eyed their intended route. They were going to need to navigate their way down more of this steep sloping forest before finally they would arrive at the long pier.

"Let's go," Davis said lifting Pedro back up into his arms once again, prompting Elena to do the same with Ariana.

They were once again on the move, proceeding down the steep hillside. As they navigated their way through the densely packed forest, Davis had them all take a ninety-degree turn. The trees in this part of the forest grew even closer together. Now they were heading more toward the interior of the island. Davis believed that they would have an easier descent down toward the long pier from this angle of attack.

They kept plowing through the forest, dodging trees left and right. Again, Davis made them take a right. Seconds later they found themselves crossing a paved road and then stepping into another small tract of forest. They made their way about another hundred feet or so through the trees and then finally at long last, they spilled out onto the long pier just as Davis had hoped they would.

But instantly Davis could see that what he hoped would in fact be here, was not. He had half expected to see a pier full of cars, shipping containers, and possibly even some boats anchored alongside the pier. Davis had hoped to find a safe spot for them all to hide and wait this long ordeal of a nightmare out. Instead, what they found was a pier devoid of any of that.

Quickly, he scanned their new surroundings. The long cement pier ran on for what had to be several hundred feet. And there at the far corner opposite to where they stood, he spotted something. It was a little difficult to make out just what it was from the distance, but Davis saw something large and green located at the far corner of the pier. It was either a large green dumpster or a big shipping container.

Needing somewhere to hide and conceal themselves, they took off in that direction. All four of them quickly got their bodies up to speed, running as fast as they could along the cement pier heading straight for the large green object at the far corner.

Davis' mind was still spinning, struggling not only to take this whole ordeal in, but struggling to gain clarity on what their next move should be. The only thing he could process at this point was that they needed to get somewhere out of view, hide for a bit, and assess what to do next.

From some unseen vantage point behind them, Davis heard a deep and rumbling cry. They needed to get out of sight ASAP.

As they closed to within fifty feet of the large object, Davis could see that it was in fact a large green metal shipping container. He had seen containers like these atop freighters traveling in the waters of the Suisun Bay from their bedroom window in the San Francisco East Bay city of Pittsburg.

"Let's position ourselves behind this thing," Davis called out to everyone.

When they arrived, they found the container to be huge, possibly close to ten feet in height and around forty feet in length. Quickly, Davis went about the task of getting his wife and kids behind it. Once he had them as safe and secure as he could manage, he'd worry what to do with himself next.

Davis now had his family positioned behind the huge container. The container itself lay several feet from the water's edge. For a split-second, Davis thought that all four of them could actually enter the water and wade out a bit. The San Francisco Bay wasn't deep at all, with about an average depth of around fourteen feet. But as he thought more about it, he realized that even if they could wade out into the cold water a bit, so too could the creatures. And the creatures currently stalking this island were huge with long powerful legs that could carry them way out into the deeper water. They would be picked off easily like a giant heron stalking fish in the shallows. Unfortunately, entering the water wasn't going to be a viable option. They stood huddled behind the mass of the container now, with their backs toward the water. With his family as safe and secure as they could be for the immediate time being, Davis headed to one of the far corners of the container to have a look what was going on back on the dock. The minute that he peeked his head around the corner of the container, his eyes were instantly greeted with movement. Lots of it. He saw people fleeing in the same direction that he and his family had just traversed, down that particular part of the hillside that led to the pier.

With the majority of his body hidden behind the large container and only his head and neck exposed, Davis watched as a man running hand in hand with what appeared to be either his wife or girlfriend suddenly tripped and fell hard to the ground. Because the two had been holding hands in a tight embrace, the man's sudden fall meant that the woman was unfortunately dragged down with him. Both could now be seen tumbling out of control end over end down the hillside. Davis could both hear and see that there were others moving in the direction of the pier as well. And then beyond the others scrambling for their lives toward the pier, Davis heard a monstrous cry announce its presence. They were being pursued and seemingly flushed in the general direction of the pier. Davis wondered to himself if it was only a matter of time before they had competition for using this huge green container as a hiding spot.

As he continued to take it all in, Davis could see that others had finally gotten themselves down off the hillside and were now running freely along the pier. Quickly, he worked his way back to his family just as the rain started to pick back up.

"Get ready," he said to the three of them. "We're not alone on the pier anymore."

The sound of another huge roar rang loud and clear. But this time it had come from much, much closer.

***

The skids of the helicopter touched down on the side of the hill as the rain continued to fall from the sky at a slashing angle. What had initially started as a gentle rain only minutes ago had quickly turned into thick rain that fell in unrelenting sheets from the sky. As the six military men dressed from head to toe in all camo gear exited the open hatch one by one, what grass there was on the hillside was beaten back and flattened by the powerful rotor-wash as the blades high above continued to thump rhythmically.

The sky suddenly lit up as lightning flashed a bright streak across the skyline. The last man exited the open hatch while thunder rumbled loudly in the distance like a bass guitar. Quickly, the helicopter began to lift up and into the rain-soaked sky before disappearing altogether back into the dark storm clouds.

Together as one, the six military men took off at a swift trot through the driving rainstorm. The wind had also picked up considerably. They moved across damp spongy ground, puddles forming and building everywhere around them.

The six men continued moving almost as if they were one, in a tight and cohesive manner, like a flock of birds. Nothing about the manner in which they moved was sloppy, nothing was inefficient. They had been given swift orders to get onto Yerba Buena Island and investigate just whatever the hell was going on. There had already been some strange calls that came in. People speaking of creatures or things patrolling the small rock of land in the middle of the San Francisco Bay. They were here to find out just what in the fuck was going on, and most importantly to prepare for the safe evacuation of those in need of help.

The thick stands of eucalyptus trees just to the left of them were really swaying back and forth now, the tops of the outstretched limbs and canopy creaking and groaning so much to the point that it seemed as though they might actually topple over at any given second.

As the six continued moving swiftly down the hillside, one of the men in the back of the line paused for a moment. The minute he brought himself to a stop, he became fully aware of just how hard the rain was coming down now, slashing and pummeling the island with reckless abandon. He had seen rain like this before, but he had to admit that it had been quite some time. Thick fat raindrops pounded down heavily onto his head and back. Turning, he thought he heard something. From back inside the dense swaying stands of eucalyptus trees there was an enormous cracking sound that rang out above even the thundering sound of the rain. It sounded like—

The soldier turned just in time to witness one of the tall swaying eucalyptus trees suddenly topple forward, forward, and forward, until finally it—

The loud *booming* impact of the one-hundred-foot-tall tree slamming hard into the ground sounded as though a bomb had just gone off. The ground itself was rocked with such crushing force that it sent a shock wave that rippled outward for a short distance.

The remaining five men spun at once. And together, the six highly trained soldiers took in the spectacular sight of the enormous, toppled tree as the rain continued to pound down atop it as well as the now exposed root system.

The original soldier that had initially stopped in the first place stood a few feet apart from the rest of the men. Through the driving sheets of rain, he saw back up the hill toward where the fallen tree now lay. Like a once great leviathan, the huge thing lay strewn a good ways down the hillside. And then the soldier's eyes flicked quickly to the left. There, laying not far from where the massive tree had been violently uprooted and toppled to the ground lay the exposed root system of the tree. What had once been a vast and extensive network of roots located underground now lay completely exposed, forming one great big ball of roots and dirt. The slashing rain was quickly turning the exposed root system into mud.

The solider continued to take it all in. But then suddenly materializing out of nowhere there was something else. An enormous shadow of a figure stepped out of the concealment of the trees and stood close to the massive root ball.

Having done two tours of duty in both Iraq and Afghanistan, the soldier had seen his fair share of true nightmarish horrors. Limbs blown off, festering wounds, shrapnel, and more bloodshed than a person would ever want to see in ten thousand lifetimes. But now here on the rain drenched hillside, through the pounding of the rain and the howling of the wind, the solider truly had no words for what he was seeing.

There, standing near the huge-exposed root system was an enormous figure. At first it was nothing more than an indistinguishable shadow. But soon whatever it was stepped forward more out into the light, exposing its ponderous bulk.

Seeing the massive sixteen-foot-tall predator standing there on its two huge powerful limbs, the soldier felt his eyes momentarily bulge forward in their sockets. And then there was a deafening wall of sound that exploded just to the right of the man as his small unit opened fire on the creature.

The sudden barrage of gunfire momentarily caught the giant creature completely off guard as a hailstorm of bullets peppered its tough and thick hide. But no sooner had the huge beast been fired upon, the powerful creature took one last look at the military men and then turned and headed back into the trees.

The lone solider drew forth his own assault rifle and immediately gave chase.

And then through the driving rainstorm the orders were shouted. "Move out, move."

Through the pounding of the rain and the sheer wind gusts, the team of six shot forward in hot pursuit of the fearsome creature. At this point, more orders and commands were being shouted out, but the rain made it impossible to hear, drowning out nearly all sounds. The rain was coming down that hard now. As they ran with their weapons pointed out in front of them, rain seemed to slash at them from all angles.

They had closed to within a hundred feet of where they initially saw the creature disappear off to, when out of nowhere an enormous figure emerged on their right side. The intense storm had momentarily concealed and masked the arrival of the huge forty-five-foot-long creature as it bore down upon them.

One of the men swung in horror and aimed his rifle up at the towering beast, unloading a torrent of bullets right into it. The assault on the creature seemed to do little to nothing as the huge, gaping maw closed down tightly around the soldier's body and lifted him from the ground. The rifle could still be heard going off from inside the creature's cavernous jaws as the huge jaw muscles and teeth crunched down upon the terrified man.

Swinging in unison, the remaining five men opened fire on the towering animal as the huge head swung up into the air and went vertical. With several massive chomps of the jaws, the beast chewed on the man for a moment before finally swallowing him down whole. Wasting no time, it turned and let loose a blood curdling roar through the rain. With eyes flaring with intensity, it eyed the remaining five men.

And then to everyone's surprise, another ungodly cry issued forth from further back up the hillside, revealing that there was in fact two of these horrific monstrosities.

Several of the men spun right there in the mud, weapons raised, aiming toward the huge, fallen eucalyptus tree. Through the thick rain, another creature emerged from the forest, opened its jaws, blaring loudly for all to hear, and charged. An animal of seemingly impossible proportions was now pounding its way down the muddy hillside toward them. The soggy, water-strewn hillside shook with the force of the creature as it neared.

***

It was hard to say at this point in time what must have officially been going on in Commander Gray Pearson's mind with the sudden reality that their current assignment now seemed nothing more than a suicide mission, a violent and bloody end that would send each and every one of them to their maker. Despite the bleakness of their situation, Pearson took two steps forward and unloaded several rounds into the charging monstrosity. The creature took the hailstorm of bullets like a tank. Letting out a deep monstrous roar there appeared to be no stopping such a primal force of nature.

Like a captain destined to go down with his ship, Commander Pearson just kept firing though. The creature seemed built more like a tank than a living breathing animal as it charged forward, shaking the ground with each thunderous step. Meanwhile, from somewhere off to the right, another deep throaty roar signified that the creature that had just killed and eaten a man was once again back on the move.

With several huge strides, the creature that had just fed was upon another one of Pearson's men in seconds. The commander turned just in time to witness the terrifyingly large animal open its huge set of jaws impossibly wide and clamp down upon one of the fleeing men. What had only minutes prior been a tight, confident, and cohesive unit, was quickly by the second being reduced to a fleeing unit of terrified, scrambling individuals.

Pearson was committed to the cause though. Wasting no time, he rushed forward toward the creature that held another one of his men captive in its fierce jaws. Nearing to within twenty-five feet of the rampaging beast, he got down on one knee and again unleashed several rounds into the massive chest cavity of the creature. He knew that they desperately needed to get a handle on things or that huge chest cavity would be all their final resting spots.

***

Somewhere in the madness of getting swept up into the crushing jaws of the big carnivore, the soldier had dropped his rifle as it clattered loudly to the ground. Still pinned tightly in place between the huge teeth, he managed to reach down to his side and unsheathe his M3 trench knife. Now with the knife firmly in his grasp, he began to stab and slash at the creature repeatedly in the front of its snout. In sharp retaliation, the creature threw its head back and forth before opening its jaws and releasing the man. The soldier fell from a height of some fifteen feet before hitting the wet ground hard. Still having the good sense about him to quickly scramble to his feet, he did just that. Armed with only his knife now, he looked up at the towering predator, the enormous mass of the creature momentarily blotting out the skyline just before the huge jaws came crashing down over him once more.

There was no time to scream, panic, or even fight back for that matter, as the immense jaws closed shut and swept him violently off the ground. The creature threw its big head back and gobbled the man down in several aggressive chomps.

***

Meanwhile, from a short distance away, Commander Gray Pearson continued to unload his rounds into the two rampaging creatures. It was quickly becoming apparent that given their current arsenal they would not be able to take whatever these things were down. Fifty feet long, with jaws larger than a full-grown man, and with a tough almost crocodilian hide that upon first glance appeared impenetrable, their options for survival on this rain-soaked hillside seemed few and far between.

Pearson kept firing on both creatures though. There was no quit in the commander, no let up, there never was. He watched with horror, though, as the creature to the left of him tracked down another one of his men. Again, he took in the sight as the huge jaws opened impossibly wide and collapsed over the fallen soldier. Spinning around in the mud, Pearson tried to take stock of who was left.

He saw nothing but the two huge creatures out away from where he stood. And then something slammed hard into his right shoulder. Spinning around, it took a moment to come to the realization that it was Mark Gonzalez and that there appeared to be no one else. They were the only two left.

Gonzalez had to yell at him to be heard over the pounding rain. "Sir, I must insist we abort. They're all gone."

Pearson scanned the hillside one last time. He saw nothing but the pounding of the rain and the powerful wind gusts, along with the tall eucalyptus trees in the far background being beaten back and forth. Beyond that he could see the two huge creatures, their massive chests filled with his men, their snouts stained with blood. Water cascaded down their tough hides in tiny waterfalls, falling to the ground relentlessly in all directions.

It was there amidst the rain and the horrors they had already seen and witnessed, that Commander Gray Pearson swore that his men would not die in vain. He would personally see to it. And with that, Pearson and his lone remaining man Gonzalez took off in an effort to take cover.

14

The storm clouds had literally stacked one atop the next, coming seemingly out of nowhere, and sending with it a torrential downpour. The rain had drenched Davis and his family to the core. Now the four of them remained huddled and cold behind the large green metal container as the unrelenting rain continued its all-out assault on the island. From somewhere far off in the background thunder rumbled.

Davis waited patiently with his family, doing his best to shield them from the rain, but at this point they were all dripping wet and soaked all the way through their clothes. With the rain coming down so hard like this, vision was momentarily obscured, and if they wanted to talk, they were forced to shout to one another.

Sloshing through the rain and puddles, Davis made his way to the end of the container once again and slowly peeked his head around. It took a moment for his eyes to take in the whole huge pier as the rain slashed and fell violently from the sky. He gave the area a good scan and saw nothing. No sign of any of the people they had heard behind them, no sign of the creatures.

No news is good news, he thought to himself, trying to ease his nerves a bit.

But the rain was coming down so hard right now he felt himself caught in the cacophony of the onslaught. Still clinging tightly to the side of the container, he peered back out toward the pier. It was a massive cement space and ran for hundreds of feet until reaching the other end, and the width of it had to be damn near fifty feet. It was quite a large area nonetheless, comprised entirely of cement.

Davis strained to see through the rain once more as it came down in thick vertical sheets. The storm was at its hardest now, pounding the island and the dock. But still he saw nothing. He found the hard rain to be beyond unnerving as it masked all sound around him. He feared that one of the creatures could ambush them, their arrival hidden by the pounding of the rain, and they would essentially have no fair warning. If that were to happen it might signal the end for-

Davis forced himself to take a deep breath. He took one last look through the rain, eyed the entire pier and surrounding hillside, and then when that turned up nothing, he sloshed his way back to Elena and the kids.

They had seen lots of people fleeing down the hillside. But in the chaos of it all, the storm, and the sheer terror that no doubt had to be coursing through each and every one of them, they had lost track of just where everyone had run off to, where everyone else had gone into hiding. Where was everyone now? Davis had no clue. All he knew was that it was still raining incredibly hard and they were all soaking wet behind the shipping container.

Having their backs to the San Francisco Bay like this, Davis couldn't help but think back to the building-sized creature that had risen up from the water near the

Bay Bridge just a few short hours ago. It was tough to get that image out of his head, tough to shake such a monstrosity from one's thoughts. The memory of that brutal encounter seemed to be seared into him like a smoldering ore. With their backs to the water like this meant that they were left in a potentially vulnerable and defenseless position. But as Davis thought more about it, he realized that if that giant monstrosity of a creature was near, they would get wind of it pretty quickly. An animal that size just walking through the bay would no doubt send huge waves coursing in all directions. If it was on the move or even in the remote vicinity of where they were, they would most definitely get a fair warning.

Davis took a deep breath and focused himself back in on his family. They needed to get out of the rain and hunker down somewhere else.

"Is it gone, Dad?" Pedro shouted through the rain.

Davis nodded and yelled back in his ear, "Yeah. At least for now it is."

"What'll we do?" Elena said, her voice shaking a bit as she spoke. "We can't keep running like this forever."

Davis tried to get his brain back online and working once again. He knew she was right. They had to take a stand or at the bare minimum avoid being detected by these creatures long enough until the appropriate help could reach the island.

"Daddy, we could always swim back home."

Despite the severity of the situation, Davis couldn't help but smile at his daughter's cute comment. "That we could, sweetie. Water's cold though and there could be sharks."

"Oh," Ariana said, seeming as though she suddenly had a change of mind. "Sharks scare me. I don't like them. They're stupid heads."

Pedro scoffed at the question. "They're top apex predators."

Ariana stuck her tongue out at her brother.

Pedro was about to reciprocate the gesture, but Davis gave his son a stern glare. Pedro kept quiet.

"Dad," Pedro said all of a sudden, grabbing his father by the shoulders. "We need to find a way to take one of these creatures down."

"How," Ariana said, folding her arms. "They're ginormous."

Ariana stuck her tongue out at Pedro once again.

Davis paused for a moment and remained deep in thought. He had to admit, Ariana may have been a few years younger than Pedro, but she sure as hell had a damn good point.

"I got a plan," Pedro suddenly yelled to his whole family as the rain continued to pound down on them.

***

Commander Gray Pearson and his lone remaining man, Officer Mark Gonzalez, continued crashing head-first through the vegetation, dodging trees left and right as they tried to put as much distance between what they had just both unfortunately witnessed out on the exposed part of the hillside a short while ago. Now they were maneuvering through the trees, both of their minds reeling with what had just transpired.

When they felt as though they had gotten themselves as far away as they could muster, Pearson raised his hand into a closed fist. Gonzalez came to a stop behind him.

Thankfully, the rain had subsided a bit, having now been replaced with a heavy thick mist that fell from the sky. Pearson and Gonzalez stood with their backs pressed up against one another as they scanned the surrounding trees. Now they were walled in tightly by dense eucalyptus growth, the huge trees shooting straight up to the sky like mini skyscraper buildings. Light availability in this part of the forest was poor at best on account of the sheer density of the trees. The tall trees here grew very close to one another.

Gritting his teeth together and doing his best to focus in on the present, Pearson scanned the section of trees that lay in front of him and to his right and left. Gonzalez was doing the same from where he stood. In what seemed like a matter of minutes, their team of six had been reduced to two. Butchered was more like it. It hadn't even been a fair fight. It was almost as if they had stumbled upon living breathing dinosaurs that had somehow managed to survive into the present day. But Pearson knew better than to believe that. The last dinosaur had walked on Earth some sixty-five million years ago. Or had it? Were these creatures oddly enough descendants of the dinosaurs? Or were they something else entirely? At this point though, he honestly didn't know the answers to these questions.

Pearson already deemed that his men would not die in vain, that he would accomplish what they set out to execute here today, and that was to successfully round up any civilians in dire straits and get them safely off the island. Suddenly, the snap of wood from somewhere close by broke Pearson from his thoughts. His eyes shot in the direction of the disturbance, his face narrowing into a fierce glare.

Several seconds of silence passed before both men could hear what sounded like a squirrel. Next, they heard tiny but sharp claws scrambling and climbing their way up one of the neighboring trees. The little creature was fast and efficient, and it was incredible just how quickly the furry animal got itself a considerable distance up the base of the tree.

Pearson just stared straight ahead though, not following the squirrel in the least bit. There were things on this island that could literally swallow a man whole. They had far bigger worries to concern themselves with instead of just a measly squirrel. Again, the snap of wood rang out from somewhere just off in the deeper parts of the brush.

Pearson had already deemed that he liked their chance of survival in here. Here, the trees grew far too close to allow a massive-bodied predator in. And if one of the creatures did in fact manage to wedge and maneuver their way in, their enormous bulk would hinder their mobility, thus allowing Pearson and Gonzalez to come in for the kill. Pearson gently stroked the trigger of his rifle as the thought of bringing one of these beasts to its knees continued to overtake his thoughts, consuming him. He pictured the enormous crashing sound of a giant body hitting the ground after he had successfully managed to kill one of these things.

Pearson steadied himself once more, his hearing and vision having gone into full-on heightened super sensitive mode. The sound of a branch breaking from somewhere high up in the canopy didn't even so much as garner a quick flinch from him. His eyes remained at ground level.

Squirrel or bird, he thought to himself, his brain operating like a finely tuned machine now.

Pearson let out a deep breath quietly through his nostrils. His pulse had slowed down next to nothing now. Without taking his eyes off the surrounding brush, he reached for one of his cigars. He didn't smoke the damn things, rather he enjoyed chewing and gnawing on them. They helped him immensely in times of great stress. And now most certainly classified as one of those times as he jammed the cigar into his mouth and immediately clenched it tightly in between his teeth.

Pearson began to rhythmically gnaw on the cigar out of the corner of his mouth. Meanwhile, from behind him, he could tell that Gonzalez was just about ready to say something when Pearson all of a sudden put his hand up in a closed fist. There was no reply from Gonzalez.

Gonzalez had heard it as well. Pearson's eyes honed-in like a hawk on the area directly in front of him. He saw the configuration of the tall eucalyptus trees growing tightly to one another. From there, the landscape started to fall away from them down a slight hill of sorts. Pearson suspected that the trees thinned a bit just up ahead. The thinning of the trees meant that they were—

The sound of something immense moving from a short distance away, confirmed Pearson's fears. Still gnawing on the cigar, a thought suddenly hit him. Certainly, these things were opportunistic hunters. For a brief moment, Pearson allowed his gaze to extend all the way up the base of one of the trees. He looked up to the top of the canopy probably a good hundred feet or so above them. And then he brought his eyes all the way back down the base of the tan-colored eucalyptus trees. Looking around for a moment, he saw the tight configuration that the trees in this small grove had chosen to exist in. Some of the tight passageways in between the trees appeared barely wide enough for a human, other areas a bit wider than that.

And then all of a sudden Pearson noticed a gentle vibration just beneath the tread of his boots. It felt as though the earth had just experienced the tiniest of earthquakes. Again, his eyes peered into the grove of tightly packed trees. He wasn't exactly certain how long the trees went on like this for. It was just that he now knew with certainty that one of the creatures was moving just beyond wherever the break in the trees existed and things opened up a bit.

Pearson drew in another deep breath through gritted teeth, the cigar still firmly clenched in between his teeth. Again, the soft ground just beneath his boots vibrated gently. Had it not been for the natural buffer of thick tree growth, they more than likely would have been knee deep in a war right about now.

We're definitely in a war, Pearson thought to himself, vengeance hard on his mind. *And war is hell.*

Point blank, Pearson now had two mission objectives. The first being to rescue and get as many people safely off this island as possible. He had already put in the call back to his base that they were requesting backup with higher fire power on account of what had already transpired. But given the direness of the situation and the fact that they were all spread so thin, he wasn't certain if that request would be met or not. All he could do now was focus in on he and Gonzalez's objectives. Coming in at a close second, was the idea of retribution for all of his men that were eaten. He certainly couldn't let them all die in vain. They died for something, they died for a worthwhile cause. He would personally see to it. He would bring as many of these beasts to their knees as he could if it was the last bloody thing he did on this Earth.

Retribution, he mumbled slowly to himself through gritted teeth. *Retribution.*

Pearson grunted quietly out of the corner of his mouth as he continued to work the wet cigar back and forth now. He paused for a moment; stopped breathing altogether. Where was the creature? What was it doing? When no further movement or noise came again, he felt his body instantly go into heightened alert mode. Were the two of them upwind or downwind? Quickly, he licked his fingertip and held it up into the air.

It took a few seconds, but eventually a slight breeze rustled through the trees. Pearson held his finger in the air a few more seconds. They were downwind. Despite their positioning, he still wondered what these creature's sense of smell was? He had spent enough company in the presence of big game over the course of his life to know just how crucial this detail in fact was. He also knew that wind direction could change at the drop of a hat.

"Guess we'll be findin' out soon enough," Pearson mumbled to himself.

A deep, shuddering sound rumbled from somewhere close by. It reminded him of the enormous sounds walruses make when breathing. It had been a terrifying thing to experience from such a close distance. The noise from just on the other side of the wall of trees had that same type of deep resonating force to it. It emphasized something of considerable size and power. Pearson unfortunately already knew all too well just what type of awe-inspiring forces of nature they were up against.

Several seconds of tense silence passed before the sound repeated itself once again.

A low rumbling bellow called out. Pearson felt the hairs on the back of his neck stand on end with the realization that the predator was just on the other side of the wall of trees as air shuddered in and out one final time. He felt another stiff breeze hit him right in the face, the wind whipping through the trees and rustling the leaves.

From beyond the trees and thick foliage the heavy guttural breathing suddenly came to a stop. A few more seconds of silence passed before both men could hear branches breaking and snapping. Something was on the move. They could hear the air as it snorted through the large nostrils now.

And then out of nowhere the direction of the wind suddenly changed on them. A stiff breeze blew at their backs, sending with it the scent of their bodies, but most importantly their location within the forest. This prompted an immediate deep snort and a grunt. The creature knew where they were now.

Again, they heard the sound of monstrous feet moving the animal forward. The creature was close now, just on the other side of the wall of trees.

Again, the wind changed directions on them. The slight breeze blew through the trees, and with it came a wave of garbage stench. For a moment, Pearson imagined that this had to be how the great predators of the past must have smelled, the great Tyrannosaurs, the Acrocanthosaurs, the Allosaurs, the fearsome predatory dinosaurs that once roamed and stalked North America all those millions upon millions of years ago. Surely this was how those great beasts from the past must have smelt, the sweet yet nauseating smell of blood, ragged chunks of flesh and entrails. The carnivores of the prehistoric past must have been great big garbage cans of putrid stench. And yet somehow, someway, here he was in the present day experiencing that same type of horrific odor as it wafted its way through the trees toward them. Whatever the hell these creatures were, they smelled unbearably bad.

Pearson quickly eyed the growth to the right and left of them. While the trees straight ahead indeed acted like a natural barrier of sorts, to the left and right of them was not as thick and a bit more spread out. This meant that it might only be a matter of time before this creature or more of its kind was able to get to Pearson and Gonzalez. The thought sent a chill down his spine, the idea of being eaten and ripped to shreds right inside the trees here. The idea of being sent straight to hell itself. He didn't fancy it one bit.

Quietly, Pearson motioned with his hand and gave the high sign for them to move out. A thick drizzle fell from the sky now and all around them the constant drip of water could be heard. The ground squelched beneath their boots as they began navigating their way through the trees.

Pearson could only hope that the ever-present sound of water dripping everywhere around them might somehow mask the noise of their progress through the forest. He wondered to himself how these creatures hunted? How was their hearing? Did they hunt by scent?

How was their vision? Whatever the tactic may have been, he knew that they along with everyone else on this island stood very little chance, if any, of ever making it off this island alive.

15

Davis Brown and his family stood huddled tightly together over a huge footprint in the mud located near the bottom of the hill not far from the storage container. Crowded in next to them were also about a dozen or so other people who had slowly started to trickle out of hiding, each staring down in both amazement and terror at the sheer size of the monstrous track in the mud.

Pedro bent down and placed his hand over the gargantuan footprint. Without touching the wet ground, he kept his hand hovering inches above the footprint, using his own tiny hand to showcase just how truly large and formidable the track was. It was big enough to literally fit his whole body inside of. These juvenile creatures appeared large enough to crush a human to death simply by stepping on them. They were that physically imposing.

"What in God's name are these things?" a man finally said, pulling back from the group and scanning up and down the hillside frantically.

"Might I also remind us all that the virus dictates that we remain six feet apart at all times. Clearly, we are in violation of that rule by being crowded in so tightly in this circle," another man replied.

A woman snorted in frustration. "Bitch please, with what we just saw, the virus is really the least of our concerns. You gotta be kiddin' me."

"I second that," another man with two kids said.

"Agreed," someone blurted out.

A stern-looking woman suddenly pulled back from the small gathering of people. Her arms were folded, her head tilted down toward the ground. Instantly, she began muttering out loud. Davis turned in the woman's direction to have a better look.

The woman just kept muttering though and backtracking until finally bringing herself to a stop. There she stood for a moment, head still drooped down toward the ground, as a barrage of gibberish continued to unload from her mouth. When she finally appeared as though she had said enough, she slowly raised her head. Making the sign of the cross fast, she seemed ready to address the small gathering of people.

"Wanna know what I think?" the woman said, her words coming fast and chaotic.

The woman once again folded her arms. A very worried and concerned look had completely overtaken her entire body at this point. "It's the devil itself. The end of days is fast upon us. I think that whatever these beasts are, they've risen from the very bowels of hell itself to put an end to us all, to put an end to mankind once and for all. That's what I think. And who could blame them? Mankind has been the scourge upon this earth for far too long now. A permanent shit stain if you will. We've had our chance as a species, failed miserably, and now maybe it's time we are wiped from existence so the earth can start anew, start fresh, clean slate and all. That's what I think."

The woman started to laugh, almost as though she could no longer hold it in, no longer control it. Childish giggles and snorts followed.

By now, each and every head that had previously been transfixed upon the enormous footprint in the mud, was staring back at the crazed woman.

The woman, still laughing uncontrollably to herself, turned her head to the side, almost as if she was having a conversation with someone that obviously wasn't there. "I know, I know, it's crazy, it's crazy. I'll tell 'em though. I'll tell 'em. Don't you worry. I will tell them everything."

A man standing next to his young son pulled both of them back as he eyed the woman. "Would you mind telling us just who in the hell you're talking to?"

The woman finished chuckling, looking over her shoulder as if someone was still there, but there was nothing more than thin air.

"I know, I know," she said in between laughs. "I will tell them, I promise. Promise."

The woman finally brought her laughter to an abrupt halt. It was incredible to literally witness someone turn the mental insanity button completely off as though it had never even happened. Her face and entire demeanor changed in the blink of an eye. No longer laughing uncontrollably while carrying on a conversation with nothing more than thin air, she had a stern look plastered across her face. A calm sense of resolve had also besieged her as well.

"It is the end, my friends," she said in an authoritative and knowledgeable tone. "The end. Plain and simple. We've had our chance, destroyed the oceans, chopped down the rainforests, absolutely obliterated the planet in every way imaginable, and now it's time we step down, thereby relinquishing our rule, and let a new species take over. It is time. This is long overdue. But it will be so much easier if we do not fight it, do not resist, and just let it happen."

Davis pulled both their kids closer to him as he eyed the woman while digesting what had just been said. While she may have been batshit looney by all outward appearances, something she said stuck with him, resonating for the time being. And that was the idea that humans had had their chance on Earth, and they'd done nothing but fuck that chance up.

"This is the end of days, my friends, and whatever these leviathans are," the woman motioned with her arms toward the enormous footprint, "certainly they are the rightful heirs to our ravaged planet Earth. And it is high time that they ascend to their throne."

The woman paused for a second to let her words soak in fully while tilting her head back and breathing in the air in deep lungful's. When she seemed as though she had breathed enough of the air in, she set her hands at her hips and addressed the small group one last time.

"My friends, there is nothing more we can do about this. The transformation has already begun. But it does not have to be something negative. Think of it as something positive. A beautiful rainbow after a long and stormy day, a larva that transforms into a butterfly. A rose that grows from a crack in the concrete. And trust me, my friends, we humans have long been that dark and stormy rain cloud on Mother Earth. We've caused nothing but misery and dread to the planet. Late is the hour, and it is much easier to accept the inevitable than to fight it. Do not fight this process that is already taking place, just let what nature has intended all along to happen. This is the will of earth."

The woman stopped speaking, folded her arms, and looked over her shoulder as she once again took up talking to no one. "There, I told them. Are you happy? See what you've done now. Just look at what you've done."

And with that she turned and began walking away from the small crowd of people still huddled closely over the enormous footprint in the mud.

"Where are you going?" someone called out to her.

The woman stopped, paused for a moment before turning around with a big smile plastered across her face. "To prepare for this transformation, of course."

16

Matt Baker knew he was on Yerba Buena Island just a short distance away from where he lived on Treasure Island. The two pieces of land are connected by a 900-foot causeway. While the actual distance itself might not have been that far, about a half a mile at most, it honestly felt like a million miles away at this point. He knew in his heart of hearts that he could make it back home to his small house enter the building, throw the door shut, and wait this nightmare out. But as he remained crouched in hiding in the bushes on the side of a large, wet, sloping hillside, he was reminded of that's not how he rolled in life. He cared about the wellbeing of others.

He readjusted himself from inside the brush as he eyed the dog not more than fifty yards from where he was. The thing had no clue whatsoever as to the potential grave danger it was in.

"Pipe down," Matt urged quietly to the barking dog. "Pipe down. Please."

The dog was standing in the middle of a large grass field, a field that for the most part was surrounded on all sides by dense tree growth. The dog was still yapping though, barking for all it was worth, to whomever or whatever might be listening.

"C'mon, c'mon, pipe down, you're killin' me," Matt mumbled nervously as he adjusted his positioning within the bushes. He had been eyeing the dog for quite some time now, wanting nothing more than to rescue and save the thing from what he knew was currently patrolling the island.

The dog yapped loudly several more times before finally craning its neck up to the sky and letting out a lonesome howling cry. It repeated this several more times.

From inside the dense matting of shrubs and vegetation, Matt had both seen and heard enough. With a great surge of adrenaline, he rose to his feet and pushed through the growth. Quickly, he extricated himself from the shrubs and took off running in the direction of the howling animal. Meanwhile, the dog with its head still tilted toward the sky and howling low moaning cries was far too preoccupied to notice the full-grown man heading its way.

Matt ran fast and low to the ground now, his legs carrying him forward in the same manner as they had done so back in his junior college baseball playing days. In one coordinated effort, he reached down and swooped the dog off the ground. The dog probably weighed a good sixty to seventy pounds in his arms as he spun around in his mad attempt to get back to where he had previously been hiding. The shaggy animal felt heavy in his arms despite the adrenaline coursing through his body.

Matt had just turned himself around and began to head for cover when he heard a series of loud cracks and the breaking of branches from deep within the trees. He flung himself around wildly just in time to witness an enormous explosion as a massive shape burst from the trees. Before he had time to process any of it, an animal that stood close to twenty feet in height and more than likely fifty feet if not longer in length was thundering toward them. The ground vibrated gently as all that tonnage thundered toward him, the creature racing out across the landscape in great, huge strides.

Literally seeing his life flashing before his eyes like scenes in a movie, Matt Baker took off with the dog at a dead sprint. He could hear the creature behind him roaring as they ran. Matt fought with all his upper body strength to hold the squirming dog off as it barked and thrashed its body back and forth in his arms. The animal seemed to have no clue the grave danger that both of them now found themselves in. Another deep, cavernous roar rang out from behind them.

Matt could see that he was fast approaching the patch of vegetation that he had previously been hiding in. But what in the hell was he going to do when he got there? Where would they go? Now nowhere seemed safe as the ground beneath them continued to shift and move.

"Shit," he cursed to himself.

Perhaps he should have thought things out better, but there was absolutely no way in good faith that he could have left the dog behind, absolutely no way. He was an animal person through and through, a lover of all things great and small. When someone or something was in need of help, you helped them, end of story. And that's just what he was doing right now. But he wondered if this random act of kindness was now going to cost him his life?

He eyed the start of the heavy brush just up ahead. He could smell the awful stench of the carnivore from close behind. It was a sweet and nauseating aroma of blood and entrails. Matt eyed the start of the dense foliage just as the squirming dog managed to wiggle right on out of his arms. At the last second, he tried to grab the barking dog with outstretched arms, but the dog quickly hit the ground running and scampered away.

The yapping of the dog was quickly drowned out by the huge predator as it unleashed another throaty rumbling sound from deep within its chest cavity. Quickly, Matt flung himself around. Staring up toward the massive creature thundering toward him, he honestly seemed at this point that despite his best efforts there was nothing more that could be done for both of them.

It felt as though it was over before it even began. The dog was going to cost him his life. Matt stepped forward, put his hands behind his back, held his head high, closed his eyes, and prepared to die. He waited as a second or two ticked by before the sounds of a barking and yapping dog caused him to open his eyes.

He opened his eyes just as the huge predator changed its intended course, planting an immense foot down and into the squishy terrain of the hillside and shifting its huge bulk. Now the gigantic creature charged in huge strides up the hillside in pursuit of the fleeing dog. The small furry yapping dog felt comically silly as the twenty-thousand-pound predator bore down upon it.

The dog, seeing what was coming its way, stood its ground though, yapping aggressively as the towering monstrosity drew nearer. When the huge creature neared to within twenty-five feet of the small and hairy feisty animal, the dog darted hard to its left. With several bounding steps, the seventy-pound animal easily avoided the charging twenty-thousand-pound creature.

Now that the dog was in full stride, it didn't stop moving. Rather, it continued darting hard to its right, almost as if it was attempting to make one great big circle around the enraged beast.

Meanwhile, the huge head with two elongated horns protruding out eyed the barking creature out of the corner of its eye as the animal continued to make a big circle around it. Somewhere in the madness of it all, the message from the giant creature's brain to its limbs must have gotten mashed and jumbled up. As the huge creature suddenly turned and lowered its head in an attempt to charge straight for the animal and pick it up off the ground in its crushing jaws, its two massive feet got tripped up. The creature tried to correct itself, but it was already too late, the slope of the hillside winning out.

The big hind leg of the creature buckled under all that weight coupled with the sudden change of direction as the giant apex predator fell hard to the ground. The enormous *boom* of all that weight hitting the ground sounded like an explosion as the hillside shook from the jarring impact. Seeing the huge fallen beast now laying on its side, the dog did not stop barking. Still continuing to bark loudly while circling, the dog was making its presence known to the fallen behemoth.

Matt Baker stood there for a moment enshrouded in silence, his mind working quickly to process what he had just seen and witnessed. He was in shock to still be alive. A creature far larger than he could have ever imagined or even dreamt up had just come bursting out of the trees in pursuit of him. He had been marked for death, yet somehow, someway still found himself alive. It was as exhilarating a feeling as he had ever experienced before in his life.

Now the huge beast lay on its side as it let out a deep, cavernous cry. Matt wondered if in its crushing fall to the ground had it injured or broken something? Perhaps. He continued to stare in disbelief for a few more seconds before finally the sound of the creature's jaws snapping closed woke him from his trance. The dog had momentarily strayed to close, causing the huge creature to raise its neck and head in an effort to kill the small animal. The dog was too fast and agile though, quickly jumping backwards, and in the process narrowly avoiding the crushing jaws of death as they snapped shut.

Matt sprung forward to life. He needed to get both himself as well as his barking companion, whom he had literally put his life on the line for, away to safety. At this point, the dog had been whipped up into an absolute frenzy and was jumping and bouncing all over the place. As Matt drew nearer, he didn't take his eyes off the huge animal for one second. He couldn't afford to.

As he pulled to within fifteen feet of the giant that now lay injured and in visible discomfort, the creature looked like a small mountain of scaly muscle and mass as it lay there sprawled out along the ground. While it had no doubt sustained a rather serious if not fatal injury to one of its big hind legs, the head and neck appeared to still be in good working order.

Matt eyed the cavernous jaws lined with giant teeth as he drew nearer. The head of the creature easily had to be six feet in length and could swallow a man whole if given the chance. He wanted nothing to do with that part of the business end of the creature. A wafting smell of garbage and shit assailed his nostrils as he drew closer.

Matt lowered himself down into an athletic position as he attempted to scoop the chaotic dog off the ground. He could smell the huge stinking creature even more now with each step he took. The jaws wreaked of dead and decaying meat, literally reeking as it if were a slaughterhouse.

"C'mon," he yelled to the dog. "We gotta go, c'mon."

Matt made a lunge for the dog, but the animal darted hard to its left. He had only taken his eyes off the huge predator that still lay sprawled on its side for a split second at best, but when he turned himself around, he watched as the huge jaws suddenly opened wide and then snapped shut, sending a pulsing wave of putrid hot breath with it.

Matt jumped hard to the left as he got the scare of his life. The jaws had come as close as an arms-length away from him. Still eyeing the massive predator, the creature was now trying to stand back to its feet. Now burdened and hindered by the enormous task of trying to lift all that weight off the ground, the predator tilted its neck and head toward the sky and let loose a blood curdling moan.

Matt refocused himself. He needed to get the dog and get the fuck out of here. They had already spent far too much time in the presence of death.

It took a moment for him to get his bearings straight, but eventually he spotted the dog in the huge grass field. It was still preoccupied with making a big circle around the fallen predator. Matt took off at a dead sprint toward the dog. Heading down the hill he passed by the huge tail that lay stretched out along the ground behind the body of the animal. As he rounded the huge backside of the terrifying creature, he got a closer look at this once-fearsome land predator. Stretching from head to tail, the creature seemed as long as a beached whale. The weight and sheer size was startling.

Meanwhile there appeared to be no stop in the dog though, barking loudly for all to hear, as it continued to make its way back around toward the huge head. Matt rounded the giant chest cavity of the creature as he eyed the dog from just a ways up ahead. The fallen creature, seeing that the small seventy-pound dog was still yapping and bouncing around, again lunged for the animal, trying to catch it in its jaws while swallowing the animal down whole. But just as it had done time and time again, the dog was able to narrowly avoid being turned into food.

As the dog backed itself up a safe distance away from the huge jaws and continued barking, Matt Baker took off full sprint toward the dog. He got there, this time completely catching the dog off guard. As he bent down and swooped the animal off the ground, cradling it tightly in his arms now, he could hear the fallen creature bellow cavernously one final time.

Matt planned on heading back to the safety of the patch of vegetation that he had been hiding in not more than ten minutes ago. Half a dozen feet or so into his journey, his ears were suddenly greeted with the staccato of gunfire. And it appeared to be coming their way.

With the barking dog still cradled tightly in his arms, Matt took off swiftly up the hillside toward the area of forest where he had initially bore witness to the arrival of the huge creature. That's where they were headed now. From there he'd assess what their next move should be.

17

Commander Gray Pearson and his lone remaining man, Officer Gonzalez, emerged from the trees with their rifles out in front of them. Pearson still held the cigar clenched tightly in the corner of his mouth as he eyed their quarry. Whatever had taken place here, seemed to have happened rather quickly. It appeared to be one series of unfortunate events after the next. But whatever had unfolded here, Pearson came to the quick realization that they just might be able to use these current circumstances to their fullest advantage. Back when they had been wedged tightly in between the safety of the trees, they had most definitely heard one of these creatures moving around. The sheer tonnage and weight of one of these things was impossible not to notice.

But now as they proceeded forward through the soaked grass and made their way out into more of the large field and toward the fallen creature, they had no way of knowing if this beast that lay before them was indeed the same creature that had been stalking the outer perimeter of the trees a short while ago. Pearson had his doubts though. It more than likely was from another member of its species. Did it really matter though? All of these things appeared to be the same—huge with no natural enemies and built seemingly indestructible like a tank. A walking set of teeth set inside monstrous jaws and powered by two enormous hind legs.

Both men took off at a swift trot. When they neared to within several dozen feet of the huge fallen mass of the animal, Pearson held up a closed fist. The two men came to a quick stop.

Suddenly, the creature's neck lifted off the ground and the big head swung in their direction. It finally noticed them standing in silence just a short distance away. A low growl emanated from its immense jaws as it eyed the two men.

From such a close-proximity, Pearson was able to truly appreciate just how breathtakingly large and imposing the animal was. In terms of overall size, it was the largest land-based animal that Pearson had ever seen in the flesh. He pulled his cigar out of his mouth for a moment and pondered the overall size and ferocity of the beast that lay sprawled out before them. His mind struggled to grapple with what his eyes were showing him.

Pearson's thoughts took him for a moment. He imagined the panic that would ensue if a full grow lion or a grizzly bear was loose in a downtown setting? The panic and sheer terror of such an event would no doubt throw a crowded area of a city into all out upheaval to know such a powerful animal was out and about. But what about the creature that lay before them? The predator had to easily weigh as much as several African elephants put together. Biting down on the cigar once again, Pearson realized that this predator was nearly nine times the size of a polar bear, currently the largest land predator on planet Earth. It was a staggering number to try and comprehend.

He continued gnawing on the wet cigar.

"What'll we do, sir?" Gonzalez asked from behind.

Pearson took one last moment to eye the entire creature from the thick, tapering tail all the way to its huge head. He could see that the animal was in visible discomfort, that was clear. The only question that remained was would the animal be able to get up under its own power or not. As Pearson took a squishy, muddy step forward, he vowed to be there to make sure that this creature never roamed the earth again. He was personally going to see to it.

A powerful gust of wind rose up from behind them, blowing at their backs before making its way down to the creature and carrying the scent of the two men with it. Almost like clockwork, the big head raised up off the ground and turned once again in their direction. The large fierce eyes homed in on them through the light mist. Another low rumbling sound emanated from its hideous maw.

Pearson seeing the huge beast with the big head raised off the ground made the blood boil inside him. These creatures had killed not only his colleagues, but his friends, and for that reason and that reason alone he wanted revenge. Pure and simple. With vengeance hard on his mind, Pearson took another step forward. Gonzalez followed.

"Don't," Pearson said through gritted teeth.

"I wanna put the bullet in that beast's belly that ends the bastard's life," Gonzalez fired back still staring straight ahead, almost in a trancelike state with his rifle leveled out in front of him.

Pearson shook his head back and forth though. "I need you here, to stand guard and watch. Understood?"

Gonzalez fidgeted nervously with the trigger of the rifle.

Pearson turned suddenly and faced his lone man, a stern look of resolve plastered squarely across his face, no emotion, no feelings whatsoever. "You're staying here. I need you to stand guard. Be alert, keep your wits about you. That's an order."

Gonzalez nodded. "And where will you be?"

"Settling the score," Pearson mumbled in a low growl. "Settling the score."

No further words were said between the two. And with that Commander Gray Pearson took off at a swift trot. The idea for the plan that he was about to execute had literally just been hashed out over the course of the last few minutes. It was a tried and proven method. It found its origins in an age-old tactic of cutting an individual, leaving him or her to die, making that person cry out for help, so that others would come, and when those others came, they would in fact be walking into the ultimate ambush attack. It was a cowardice tactic in every sense of the term. But over the course of his career, Pearson learned something of the upmost importance, and it stuck with him on each and every mission that he had been a part of. No matter where in the world he might have found himself, no matter what the mission might have been. It was stunningly simple but all too brutally real. And that was, that in battle there is no law. Do whatever you had to do in order to survive. That was all that mattered now.

Pearson went from a swift trot to a full-on sprint. And just like the frames and scenes of a movie, bits and pieces of what he was about to execute began to flash in his head at rapid fire. As he neared to within fifteen feet, a thick wall of stench rose up to greet him. Making a round arc, his eyes focused in on the enormous chest cavity of the creature. A fierce bellowing roar sent a wave of hot stinking breath his way as the creature lifted its head and neck from the ground and turned and faced in the direction of the attacking solider.

Pearson, fully committed to the cause at this point, paid absolutely no attention whatsoever to the powerful neck and the big head as it turned and lunged for him. Laying his rifle down carefully in the wet grass he quickly unsheathed the Ka-bar knife at his side. He took off at a dead sprint. And then with everything he had, he sent himself catapulting up and into the air.

Pearson sailed through the air, landing near the top of the creature's heavily muscled back. Using every last bit of his strength, he managed to perch where he was against the thick hide of the creature just long enough to lift the knife over his head, and then with every ounce of strength he could muster, sent it plunging straight into the creature. Pushing through the tough hide and sinewy muscle he could only manage to jam the knife several inches at best. It would have to do.

With his feet still holding him up against the side of the huge chest cavity, Pearson suddenly pushed off with both feet. Now with two hands firmly atop the handle to the knife, Pearson fell downward almost as if he was repelling down the side of a mountain. As he fell downward, he brought the knife still plunged into the side of creature with him. It tore a ragged gash into the side of the beast. By the time Pearson finally brought himself to a stop, the bleeding gash had to be damn near five feet in length.

If the giant predator had failed to notice the Ka-bar knife plunging into its side before, it most definitely felt the five-foot-long ragged gash that had ripped its side wide open now. Letting out a blood curdling scream, it threw its head and neck back and forth in a violent whipping motion. And in doing so, the massive predator threw Pearson off in the process. Pearson was thrown hard to the ground as the creature bucked itself back and forth like an overgrown bronco. He hit the ground rolling, immediately scrambling to his feet in an effort to locate his rifle. It took him a second or two, but he quickly got his bearings straight as he sheathed the knife at his side.

He retrieved the automatic rifle from the ground just as the enormous creature let loose a monstrous screaming cry. From the pain of having just been ripped wide open along its side, the creature let loose another ungodly cry that seemed as though it had come from another time in Earth's history entirely. As Pearson back peddled now, wielding the rifle out in front of him, he had been to the Serengeti in Africa on several assignments to know just what the sound of a wounded animal sounded like.

As he began circling the huge animal laying on its side sprawled about on the ground like the wreckage of a downed plane, he knew that the behemoth was slowing bleeding out. Pearson reached into the pockets of his vest and retrieved several small black objects. Now rounding the backside of the creature, he could see the huge tail snaked along the ground, lying in a growing pool of blood that had already stained the wet grass. He strategically placed one of the small black boxes on the ground at the tip of the huge tail. He continued moving though, there wasn't a moment to spare.

Out of nowhere, the massive carnivore let loose another deep and throaty moaning roar. This time the cry rattled his body. Pearson was moving even faster now. Heading to the right side of the animal just behind the huge gut of the creature, he placed another one of the black boxes down onto the ground, as close to the rough pebbled hide of the creature as he could.

Pearson quickly stood back up as he rounded toward the long neck and the big head. The creature must have heard his footsteps, quiet as they may have been, because it immediately lifted its head and swung it in the direction of the commander. Pearson felt the animal's hot breath as he jumped backwards just at the last second to avoid the huge rows of teeth. The top part of the jaw slammed shut to the join the bottom part. There was a sickening sound of giant teeth—each the size of bananas—colliding with one another. The creature eyed Pearson and let loose a rumbling bellow just as the man set another small explosive box some five feet from the huge head.

Pearson wasn't done though. Still moving swiftly and with a sense of absolute purpose, he made his way toward the side of the creature where he had initially launched his brutal attack. He paused for a second to take in the bleeding gash running down the side of the huge chest cavity.

Pearson got right up next to the side of the animal and set the fourth and final explosive in place. Once it was down and nestled in the soggy ground, he quickly began scrambling his way back toward Gonzalez.

***

"Holy shit," a man blurted out as he pulled away from the group still huddled close to the enormous three-toed footprint in the mud.

"Hey, watch your mouth," a woman fired back, doing her best to shield her young daughter's ears from the curse word.

"Hey, listen lady," the man retaliated, swinging his arms in the air. "We got much bigger problems on our hands now. Much bigger problems. Are you hearing this shit?"

No sooner than he had spoken those very words, another immense cry suddenly filled the air, prompting Davis to look back up the hillside, toward the dense stands of eucalyptus trees. As he did so, he watched as a dozen or so black ravens squawked loudly as they shot off from the tops of the trees and lifted themselves high into the air.

"They can smell death everywhere," a voice said in an eerie almost inhuman tone. "They're attuned to what's going on. The question is, are you?"

Davis and the others brought their gaze down from the sky and saw once again that the religious woman had returned. This time she had something clasped tightly to her chest. It took a moment but eventually she opened the bible up.

"The end of days has been documented in the word of God." She now spoke in a calm yet authoritative tone. "Have you all been saved by Jesus Christ, my lord and savior?"

Davis eyed his wife for a brief yet intense embrace. Slowly, they grabbed both kids and began to backtrack away from the group. Meanwhile the woman still holding the bible out in front of her, quickly noticed the family of four slowly trying to extricate themselves from the situation.

"Ah," she said in a loud and sarcastic tone pointing. "I see we have some non-believers. The word of God isn't for everyone, but just know that should you all perish on this island before you have indeed been saved, then you and your family, sir, will all burn in the fires of hell. This we know with certainty."

The woman instantly dropped her gaze from Davis and his family and began muttering indecipherable words as she continued to read from the very pages of the bible that she still held in her hands.

"Where to now?" Elena asked nervously.

"Dad, anywhere but here," Pedro said.

"Agreed," Davis replied, while having a quick look around.

"Daddy, I'm scared. That woman's scary. She's like a witch or something" Ariana blurted out.

"Not to mention looney," Pedro added.

The four continued backtracking as the woman closed the bible shut loudly.

"You know," the woman said as she addressed the group once again. "There's always another route. God can be appeased, perhaps momentarily diverting his attention from his true task at hand, allowing you all to get off this tiny rock of an island with your lives."

The woman paused for a moment, bible still clasped firmly against her chest almost as if it were her child. She paused and waited in silence.

"Go on with it?" someone shouted.

The woman held off for a few more seconds before finally hissing out the words as though she were a serpent. "A sacrifice."

The woman began to make her way back to where the others stood, still hovering close to the enormous footprint in the mud. Quickly, she began eyeing each and every one of them. Her gaze twitched back and forth furiously, looking at each one of them like a predator eyes its prey. She went from the adults of the group to that of the young children.

"A child," she hissed again, her voice having suddenly taken on a serpent almost snake-like quality about it. "The sacrifice of a child to appease God."

Immediately, all the kids that had been hovering close to their parents' legs, suddenly turned and hid their faces from the woman, not wanting to see her as she crouched low to the ground to have a better look at each and every one of them.

The woman made her way until she finally stood in the middle of the small circle of people. With her head down she stared at the enormous track. And then she placed her feet right into the middle of the footprint itself, her shoes instantly sinking down into the soft squishy mud. Now she stood in the middle of the huge footprint that dwarfed her.

The woman continued. "These creatures will not stop, will not rest until they have feasted on every last one of us. Do you all want this to be your fate? That is why it is imperative that we must do something."

The children in the group still stood with their backs to the woman. Some buried their heads in their hands, wanting nothing more than to probably disappear at this point.

"God is the powerful almighty creator of all, and I have no doubt that he played a hand in creating these magnificent beasts of death and destruction. But while God's wrath can be devastating and savage at times, I have no doubt that he is also a just and deserving God. Which is why me must sacrifice one of our own. We must spill the blood."

The woman paused. Both her feet were still sunk down several inches into the mud, the huge-clawed footprint only to serve as a sense of scale as to just how large and imposing the creatures that had invaded the tiny island in fact were.

"Don't think that this is all that you will face on this island. There are nightmares far worse than what you have already seen and experienced. For there is a living monstrosity that bore down upon the San Francisco-Oakland Bay Bridge earlier this morning. And it's just out yonder now patrolling the waters around San Francisco right this very minute. It's as big as a building is large, I tell you. These creatures that you see on this island are its magnificent offspring, its young."

"Bullshit," a man replied as he spat. "You're tellin' me these huge creatures on this island are infants."

The woman nodded. "Essentially yes."

Another man shook his head back and forth. "No way. You're spewing complete bullshit to all these people. Getting them worked up into a frenzy. Not buying it."

The religious woman merely nodded. "Swear words are not necessary in the presence of all these young children. I can also assure you that God does not play games when it comes to issues surrounding life and death. This monstrous creature I speak of is indeed very real, and if it does decide to make landfall, it has the ability to send humans back to the stone ages. Its wrath of destruction will make the creatures on this island seem like child's play."

This time no one in the group said a word. All was quiet as they struggled to take in what the woman had just said.

"She's right," a man finally said stepping back from the group while holding up his cell phone. "She's right at least about a creature the size of a building."

"Wait," a woman said. "You have cell service?"

The man shook his head. "No. Towers are down or something. I don't think anyone here as cell service, but I managed to film this footage earlier today just before part of the bridge collapsed."

Quickly, the majority of the people began to make their way toward the man. He wasted no time as he brought up his videos on the phone and began to play the footage he had captured earlier in the day. No one said a word as they watched the man filming the monstrous creature from the safety of just inside the tunnel as the creature raised its limbs and tore away at part of the bridge.

"With his footage perhaps now we all can go from being non-believers to believers. And while I would have appreciated you all believing me simply on my word, I do understand that sometimes these matters take time," the religious woman spoke. "Now if you all can place your full trust in me, we have some very important matters that need to be addressed."

A woman stepped away from the small gathering of people still huddled closely over the man's phone. "How 'bout we sacrifice you. At this stage of the game a sacrifice is a sacrifice, flesh is flesh. Besides you're more of a meal anyway, more meat on the bone."

The religious woman seemed taken aback at the comment as she stumbled backwards a few feet. "Well, that's, that's not how these matters work, I can assure you."

A few people broke away from the group now and stood behind the first woman who stood as a direct threat to the religious woman's plans.

"Lady, if you want a sacrifice," a man said, "then I side with this woman here. Why don't we sacrifice your ass?"

The majority of the group cheered the man's harsh words.

Taking in a big breath of air, as if soaking in the very words that she had just spoken, the woman suddenly spun in the mud and eyed Davis and his family as they continued to make their way.

"There," she hissed pointing to Davis Brown and his family. The four of them could now be seen scampering their way back up the green hillside.

"Get them. The hell with it. Bring me both children. We'll sacrifice both, doubling our chances for getting off this island with our lives. Now bring them to me," she roared at the top of her lungs.

And it was there, in that moment, on the tiny island not far from San Francisco that a general sense of madness and isolation had set in. A loud crack of thunder could be heard from not too far off in the distance as dark storm clouds continued to stack one on top of the next. Just as a small group of people took off in hot pursuit of the family of four, fat heavy raindrops began to fall from the sky.

18

M att Baker and his new four-legged companion had heard every bit the disturbance to the surrounding trees all around them as both he and the dog continued trudging up the hill. The dead weight of the dog was starting to weigh him down a bit now, but Matt didn't want the dog wandering off like it had before. He couldn't afford for that to happen again. Matt wanted to put as much distance in between themselves and the downed carnivore back in the middle of the large grass field as possible. But as the two pushed further and further into the thick grove of trees, maneuvering their way through the giant trees, they heard immense cracking sounds from all around them. The sound of wood being broken and splintered rang out loudly from all sides. It felt as though they were surrounded, the forest itself quickly closing in and converging on them.

Matt didn't stop though. He knew they couldn't afford to at this juncture. Rather, he just kept pushing further and further up the hillside as sounds of the forest being broken and battered rang out from what seemed like all sides of them. He knew what it possibly meant.

Cannibalism, he thought to himself as he forced both he and the dog through a rather tight opening in between two trees. The downed giant back in the large grass field was no doubt attracting other predators in the area, much like a dead whale carcass attracts scores and scores of sharks.

Blood in the water, he thought, scraping both his arms on the trees. He emerged from the tight growth only to see that just a short-ways away up ahead, some sort of dangling green ivy could be seen. The ivy draped itself and grew over one of the large limbs from high above, forming what could best be described as a curtain of green matting. Matt and the dog were moving too fast at this point though to reroute themselves. With the full weight of the dog still cradled tightly in his arms, they went plunging head-first through the draping wall of ivy.

For what seemed like a short eternity, Matt just kept plowing his way through the long, draping growth. There appeared to be no end to it. He pushed forward though. And then finally at long last, as both he and the dog emerged out from the ivy, his eyes took in a rather unsettling sight. Probably a good twenty-five yards up the hill, the trees formed a large tunnel of growth walled in on both sides by dense trees and thick underbrush.

The ground shook now with what lay up ahead at the end of the tunnel of trees. Matt felt his stomach drop as he saw a monstrous form charging straight for them, mouth agape, ropes of saliva flying off the huge, glistening, serrated teeth. The creature was blaring loudly for all to hear. The tunnel of trees was just large enough for the terrifying animal to maneuver and move its way through.

Charging full force toward them and roaring like an out-of-control freight train Matt hardly had any time to mount a corrected course of action. Both he and the dog were about to be steamrolled.

At the very last second, Matt launched both he and the dog as close to the base of one of the trees as he could. He slammed his body and the dog right up against the big tree, grabbing, and hugging it for all it was worth as the huge mass of the creature went barreling on right past them.

Craning his neck to the side he caught a quick glimpse of the creature. He saw the massively long clawed front limbs, huge powerful legs powering the beast forward, followed by a long and muscular tail meant to counter-balance the immense weight. He watched as the spiked tail passed right on by them. The fearsome predator bellowed a deep rumbling cry.

Out of the corner of his left eye, Matt watched as the great weight of the creature rushed on by him. Turning in stunned disbelief that they had even managed to survive such an encounter, Matt watched as the creature continued plowing its way through the tunnel of trees.

The towering beast and the big head had hardly so much as even noticed them as it continued onward. It could have only meant one thing. Something else was on the menu; something far, far larger and more substantial. One of their own was about to be cannibalized.

Another gaping roar exploded from the creature's immense jaws as the enormous animal plunged headfirst through the draping ivy before finally disappearing on the other side. The sound of its heavy feet continued for a while longer before all evidence of its presence in this forest was gone. Silence once again returned to the forest.

For a moment, Matt and the dog just stood there, pinned up tightly against the tree, breathing hard. He was in total shock and disbelief at what had just transpired. It honestly felt like a twenty-foot-long great white shark had suddenly brushed by his surfboard only to disappear down into the murky depths below. Matt took a much-needed moment to catch his breath. He was breathing hard, and it took him several seconds to regain himself to the point where it felt like his brain was finally back online.

Slowly, his thoughts started to come to him. Certainly, the animal was headed back to the large clearing where the injured creature lay. It was the only logical explanation he could come up with as to why he and the dog hadn't been scooped up in the crushing jaws and eaten alive. Whatever the reason was though, he was beyond grateful to still be alive, to still have a chance to get both himself as well as the dog to safety. And he wasn't about to waste their second chance at life.

For a moment he stared back through the long tunnel of trees, half expecting to see the creature emerge through the draping wall of ivy and begin to bear down on them once again. And then suddenly he felt a warm sensation to the bottom of his chin and neck. It took a moment but eventually he looked down and saw the dog licking him. He had forgotten that he was even holding the animal in the first place. The dog continued to lick him for a few seconds longer before looking up at him with big and sympathetic eyes. Matt stared into his new companion's eyes for a while longer. And it was there in the dog's eyes, nestled at the base of a giant eucalyptus tree, that Matt Baker came to understand that the dog represented hope to him, plain and simple. He felt he needed the dog as much as it needed him.

"I think I'll call you Hope," Matt said stroking the animal's head. "Yeah, Hope it is. As long as that's okay with you?"

The dog barked and wagged its tail back and forth.

"It's settled then; from now on you shall be Hope."

The dog licked the bottom of his chin once more. He smiled as he looked down at the animal. And then his eyes shot up the corridor in between the trees toward where they first laid eyes on the rampaging creature. They needed to get back up the hill, through the rest of this forest, and to the other side of the island. And they needed to do it quickly, but most importantly stealthily, traveling out of sight and under the radar.

Matt knew there was a new high story luxury apartment complex or possibly condos that had recently started to pop up on the right side of the Bay Bridge as you were driving into San Francisco. If they could just manage to get to the construction site, they could possibly seek some sort of temporary shelter there.

The building was a long way away from being complete though. But Matt was thinking that he and Hope could scamper their way up to the higher levels. He remembered that he had been driving across the bridge into the city a few months ago when he had seen the new development literally pop up out of nowhere. In the following months it was just this plain gray cement construction, but in recent weeks it had been blanketed by huge white tarps. If he could just get the two of them to the construction site, they could either seek refuge inside the confines or find a staircase that'd put them in a higher and hopefully safer location. Anywhere was better than their current location.

He turned around for a moment and stared back to the draping ivy that hung from a large network of crisscrossing branches some twenty feet up. The forest had also suddenly fallen still and quiet. Matt heard a few birds chirping softly to one another from somewhere higher up in the canopy. Other than that, things were eerily quiet. Too quiet. He turned and faced in the direction they needed to head to. Letting out a deep breath he stared down at Hope.

"Okay, you ready to do this?"

Matt set Hope down on the ground. The dog barked as it wagged its tail.

Matt smiled. "Thanks, I needed that."

And with that the two took off.

***

Commander Gray Pearson finally managed to scramble his way back to Gonzalez who was still standing guard just at the edge of the thick tree line. Pearson made no eye contact with Gonzalez, rather his eyes were sweeping back and forth to the solid wall of trees that bordered this large grass field. With the dying sounds of the creature moaning out for all to hear, he knew it wouldn't be long now. It was only a matter of time before the rest of the apex predators currently patrolling this tiny island officially took notice, if they hadn't already. They would come in droves, driven forward by their seemingly insatiable appetites. Driven forward by the prospect of a fresh a kill, of big ragged bloody chunks of fresh meat.

Just as the rain had started to pick back up, so too did the wind, whipping the tops of the trees some hundred feet above them back and forth now. The eerie sounds of massive trees creaking, groaning, and cracking from side to side dominated the huge grass field now. As

Pearson continued scanning, it felt as though the whole island was slowly coming alive on them.

"Over there, sir," Gonzalez pointed.

Pearson swung his rifle around just in time to see two enormous figures step out from the rain-soaked trees that lined the opposite side of the clearing. Both creatures stood fully exposed as the rain continued to pound down on them, small streams of cascading waterfalls running down and across their thick pebbled hides. The two big heads remained ever present and watchful, towering above the ground, eyeing their quarry.

Pearson reached into his vest and retrieved his monocular. Now staring through it with his right eye, he saw the two giant creatures on the other side of the huge grass field. The larger of the two stepped forward through the rain. Through the monocular, Pearson saw the thick hind limbs that carried the creature's tremendous weight. Extended outward and waving back and forth was the huge tail ending in four sharp and pronounced spikes. He also eyed the big head, and the two fearsome horns that shot out like the horns of a bull.

Pearson wondered to himself for a moment what the purpose of the spiked tail and the horns were for? He knew that creatures such as Stegosaurus had spiked tails as a form of protection from potential predators. Was the design of this creature before him employing the very same tactic? Did these animals also gore their prey with their horns? He didn't know the answer to either question.

Still staring through the monocular Pearson continued moving across the immense body. He saw the toes and the fingers each adorned with large black oversized claws. He made his way back to the head of the creature, focusing in on the great jaws, anchored in place by tremendous muscles. The huge jaws sat slightly agape, allowing Pearson a better look at the dentition of the beast. Zooming in as best he could with the monocular, he peered into the enormous jaws, and could see that the huge teeth were sharp, curved, and serrated for the tearing of flesh.

Though he would never admit it to anyone—it wasn't part of the nature of his line of work—Pearson shuddered quietly to himself for a moment, knowing the fateful end that four of his men had suffered at the hands of these horrific things. Massive and with seemingly no natural enemies, it was as brutal an end to a human life as one could ever imagine. He continued to take in the last of the two rain-soaked beasts still standing just at the edge of the trees.

They did not die in vain. They died for something, he thought to himself, the memory of his men still hard on his mind.

An ungodly cry of pain rang out, breaking him from his thoughts, and prompting Pearson to immediately lower the monocular. His gaze went from the two hungry predators at the edge of the tree line to the dying, agonizing moan of the creature that still lay on its side bleeding to death in the middle of the large field. Pearson eyed the injured animal. He could see the bleeding gouge from his knife that had ripped a gash into the side of the beast's great chest cavity. Now that gash was pulsing a steady yet consistent flow of crimson red blood. Pearson had just looked down to the small yet growing pool of blood that the creature now lay in, when suddenly he caught movement out of the corner of his left eye.

Silently and stealthily, the two creatures at the far end of the clearing moved forward toward the fallen behemoth. The larger of the two predators arrived at the creature's side first. Wasting no time, it made its way to the pulsing five-foot long gash, and placed its long, oversized, clawed front limbs down atop the side of the animal. The claws that lined the two limbs gripped down onto the thick hide of the animal. And then in an aggressive move, the creature dragged the claws down the side of the animal. Huge, oversized claws gripped and dug into the thick hide, tearing and raking long gouging marks into the flesh of the animal.

Pearson and Gonzalez took in the growing and unfolding scene as the wind continued to whip the towering trees at their backs. Pearson took a few steps away from Gonzalez now and turned himself around just as one final death cry could be heard as the two creatures tore into the bleeding animal. Pearson wasn't paying attention though. He stared intently back at the swaying stand of trees behind them.

It took a moment, but Pearson thought he had heard something from the trees at their backs. Another few seconds passed before Gonzalez spoke.

"Over there, sir," Gonzalez said pointing through the rain.

At the top of the clearing, two more enormous figures dragged their rain-soaked bodies through the last of the trees and emerged out into the open. They took off through the rain, making their way down the sloping grass hillside toward where the other two of their kind were busy feasting on the warm carcass.

The once mighty carnivore that now lay on its side in the long grass had been completely ripped open by the time the other two predators finally arrived on the scene.

Wasting no time, they tore into the body, each huge animal focusing in on a particular piece and quickly working and pulling off muscle and gore in great, huge chunks. With the snouts of their jaws now stained red, in a matter of minutes what had once been an enormous chest cavity, had suddenly been ripped wide open. Now the massive, curved ribs of the beast lay open and exposed as the rain continued coming down.

Pearson motioned to Gonzalez. Together the two began moving toward the bottom of the clearing. At the very bottom of the clearing, the trees that ringed this part grew densely and tightly packed. Pearson's eyes quickly flicked to the right just to give a quick scan that nothing else was coming out of the trees and entering the large field with them.

Pearson motioned with his rifle for Gonzalez to put a set of eyes on those trees though. They most certainly couldn't afford for anything with a huge mouth lined with teeth and an equally massive appetite to come waltzing right on in here unannounced.

Pearson eyed the four huge feeding predators for a few seconds longer before finally taking one last sweeping view of the entire field. At least for the moment nothing else was emerging out into the open to feed. Four giant feasting predators appeared to be the final number.

He had just reached into his vest to retrieve the detonator. He didn't have much time. A quick glance back to the ravaged bloody carcass revealed that the four huge predators were well more than halfway done with the meal. They had torn the body of the giant carnivore wide open, the huge chest cavity and the giant bones that formed the ribcage now lay completely open and exposed. It was an absolutely sickening sight and it wouldn't be long now until there was nothing more than random pieces of skin and flesh clinging tightly to bone here and there. Pearson had to act quickly.

He reached back and tapped Gonzalez on the shoulder. His man still had eyes on the trees behind them. Gonzalez turned around. Pearson held the detonator up and made eye contact with Gonzalez. Not a word was said between the two though, as Pearson turned back around, detonator in his right hand, ready to inflict maximum damage on these creatures at the push of a button. He had every intention of sending them straight to hell in giant chunks and pieces.

Pearson studied the four feeding carnivores for a further few seconds. Animals so large and massive that the ground literally vibrated and shook each time they were on the move. And then that sense of awe and wonder turned into hate as the thought of the way that each of his four men had been killed and dismembered at the hands of these beats came rushing back to him. The way they had been systemically dismantled and killed was nothing short of pure savagery.

Pearson held the detonator now out in front of him. The muscles in his face bunched and tightened into that of a permanent scowl. With no warning, one of the creatures lifted its head from the ravaged bloody carcass and turned and looked back toward the two men. Meat and loose entrails hung from the lower jaw of the creature's blood-stained snout.

This prompted the other three creatures to lift their enormous heads as well. Pearson and Gonzalez had been spotted. Two creatures remained with heavy limbs and clawed feet pressing down and into the side of the carcass as they continued to eye the two-armed men.

Putting no further thought into it, Pearson pushed the button on the electronic detonator.

19

The explosion rocked the small Yerba Buena Island, sounding for a precious few seconds as though a bomb had literally just gone off in the middle of the San Francisco Bay. Given the size and scale of the tiny island, it may as well have been a bomb.

Davis and his family were once again on the move. He wasn't certain exactly what had transpired with the religious woman and the small crowd of people back near the enormous footprint in the mud. All he knew with certainty was that he got his family moving the minute he saw the religious woman point out and bring them to the attention of the gathering of people.

Pushing furiously through the eucalyptus trees now, he had no clue if anyone was following in pursuit of them or not. All he knew was that he wanted to get them as far away from that area as possible. They saw light that marked the huge field just up ahead. Pedro was running side by side next to his dad now. Meanwhile in front of them Elena was carrying Ariana in her arms. Elena's long and fit runner legs carried her through the trees now, weaving and zigzagging through the huge trunks, pushing onward toward the lit clearing.

***

Commander Gray Pearson and Mark Gonzalez took off moving swiftly through the large grass field. When the blast had initially gone off, both he and Gonzalez had managed to put several hundred feet of separation in between themselves and ground zero. Still though, despite the distance, they had been close enough to feel the intense heat from the explosion.

As they ran toward the tall swaying trees that bordered the right side of the clearing, moving about through the long-wet grass, huge chunks of meat and gore rained down all around them. To Pearson it honestly felt like a sadistic battlefield, with limbs, tails, and all sorts of other body parts hitting the ground with loud and resounding SPLATS. Already, great big swaths of blood had streaked and stained the grass that made up the field.

Paying no attention to the falling chunks of flesh and muscle that continued to rain down all around them, they kept moving swiftly toward the tall stand of trees. It wasn't until the burnt and charred remains of a huge back limb from one of the creatures slammed down right in front of them not more than twenty feet from where they were running, that the ramifications of what the detonator and four explosives had pulled off came full circle on them.

As they ran past the enormous back hind limb, it was hard not to take in the horrific sight. The tough, leathery hide of the giant body part was burned and charred in spots almost making it unrecognizable, but what was recognizable was the size and mass to the big leg along with the huge claws at the end of the three-toed foot. Easily as wide around as a small tree, had the limb in fact hit them, they would have more than likely been killed on the spot. It was that massive.

Pearson couldn't help but take in the huge, clawed toes of the animal. The clawed toes were absolutely enormous, meant for tearing and ripping things apart with sheer brute strength. They only served to further emphasize the devastating weaponry that each of these horrific beasts came equipped with.

Pearson took one last look back to the big hind limb ending in massively constructed thick oversized black claws. And with that he turned and quickly headed for Gonzalez who was nearing the tall stands of eucalyptus trees. By now, there was nothing left falling from the sky. The bloody body parts, bones, and entrails were now scattered about all over the large grass field in what could only best be described as pure hell itself.

Meanwhile from a short distance up ahead, Pearson watched as Gonzalez finally disappeared behind a row of trees. And with that, Pearson picked up his own pace and headed for the cover of the trees.

20

M att Baker and Hope exited the last of the forest. They crossed a small, paved road and began carefully making their way along a dirt trail that was lined on both sides by cyclone fencing. This part of the island had massive construction going on as of late. Matt knew where they were headed though. They were heading back toward the Bay Bridge. Hope was out in front of him leading the way as they walked the narrow path. Another few steps or so passed by before they were able to see hundreds of cars still parked along the bridge.

Matt had planned for them to traverse a steep hillside that would lead them back onto the bridge. Parts of this island at times lay flush against the bridge itself, thus allowing the possibility for one to move to and from. The steep hillside lay far from the tunnel that ran through the island, and it was that hillside that Matt planned to navigate across in order to get them back on the bridge. From there they'd be able to cross the bridge and step over the fencing on the other side to where the newly constructed upscale building was being built.

A distinct snort and a grunt brought both Matt and Hope to a stop. The two of them waited and listened.

There it was again, the-all too familiar sound that could have come from one animal and one animal only. Matt heard a low bellowing rumble. The sound itself amplified and echoed off the walls and ceiling of the tunnel. Not far from where he stood one of the creatures must have been in the-

Shit, he cursed silently to himself. *Fuck. What now?*

The dog turned itself around, looked up at her new owner with big and sympathetic eyes, and began to wag her tail back and forth while panting, almost as if waiting for his command. Matt had just bent down to grab hold of Hope, when up ahead his eyes locked in on a tail as it came into view. From his vantage point still on the island, he really didn't have the proper view back into the tunnel that sat on the bridge. But he still was able to see a huge tail as it momentarily came into view, peeking its way out of the tunnel if only for a few seconds.

Matt looked down at Hope and motioned for her to be quiet. She stood there wagging her tail silently, mouth open, tongue visible. Neither of them made a sound though. Another sharp reverberating grunt echoed from up ahead in the tunnel. Matt assumed that the predator couldn't see them. But they were close, nonetheless.

Again, Matt eyed the start to the tunnel. He didn't see anything. And then suddenly he watched as a large head partially emerged from the tunnel. The big head froze in place. Matt could hear his heart beating now as it pounded against his rib cage. The big head remained absolutely still, perhaps staring out of the tunnel back at the parked cars all stuck in place.

"C'mon," Matt said reaching down to pick up Hope once again. "C'mon. We can't stay here. Gotta get goin'."

Quietly and unassumingly, they began to make their way back from where they had just come from. They needed to get back down a ways, about a few hundred feet or so, and then hang a sharp right. From there they would make their way past a boarded up white home that sat high above a small road and scamper their way across the hillside that grew atop the tunnel. All they needed to do now was get over that small hillside and they would essentially be on the other side of the island, the correct side they needed to be on in order to hide and take refuge in the building that was currently under construction. With those thoughts in mind, Matt and Hope continued on their way.

***

Davis and Pedro could see Elena and Ariana up ahead. The two were standing just at the edge of the tree line, and beyond that, they could see a huge grass field that sloped downward at an angle. As Davis drew closer, he could in fact see just how big the field was. It was a huge grass field spanning hundreds of feet.

"C'mon, Dad," Pedro said as he edged past his father.

The two kept running, weaving their way in between the towering eucalyptus trees before finally reaching Elena and Ariana. While father and son were both breathing hard, chests heaving in and out, Elena and Ariana seemed as cool as a cucumber, hardly even so much as breathing.

"Well," Elena said with a wide smile across her face. "Guess we know which two of us are the far superior athletes."

"Girls," Ariana blurted as she stuck her tongue out at Pedro.

The statement drew a laugh from both Davis as well as Pedro. It felt good to crack a smile, it really did. They all needed the laugh, even if it was short lived.

"See," Ariana said proudly as she folded her arms. "Told you girls are better than boys."

But try as he may, Pedro was still an eight-year-old boy, and no self-respecting eight-year-old boy was going to sit back and get clowned on by their younger sister. It just wasn't going to happen. Pedro stuck his tongue out in sharp protest at his sister's comments. As much as Davis both needed and appreciated the small window of laughter, they weren't going to get that break. Shit was happening too fast in real time to even sit back and catch one's breath at this point.

"Dad," Pedro said suddenly, his small chest heaving in and out. "Remember that small building that started to be built just on the right side of the bridge as you're heading into the city?"

Davis nodded as he looked behind them and did a quick sweep with his eyes. He saw nothing, only heard the wind as a stiff breeze blew through the trees and rustled the foliage and shrubs at the ground level.

"Dad," Pedro said slapping Davis on the leg. "Dad, we need to get our asses to that building. Climb to the top of it. Wave and shout for help or at least, be safe up there."

"Hey, watch your mouth young man," Elena said pointing at her son. "What've I told you about swearing."

Elena glared at Davis for a moment, telling him with her eyes that his years of swearing and foul language was finally starting to catch up with him; rub off on their kids. But the gears were already churning upstairs for Davis. Of course, he remembered the building Pedro was talking about. How could he not. The thing seemed to have shot up literally overnight. Plus, the fact that it had been his goal to get into selling commercial real-estate. He had also been toying back and forth with the idea of earning his real-estate license for several years now. But like so many other things he had momentarily put it on the back burner.

"Dad," Pedro said beating his hands against Davis' legs. "Dad."

Out of nowhere a sharp and distinct cracking sound suddenly rang out from somewhere back in and amongst the trees. Davis turned in that direction. Next, they heard voices, followed by the sound of feet crunching down atop dead leaves. All this noise appeared to be heading in their direction.

Horror gripped Davis at the first glimpse of heads bobbing back and forth making their way through the trees in pursuit of them.

Shit, Davis thought to himself, knowing that this surely had to be the work of the religious woman back near the huge footprint in the mud. Were these individuals out to do her dirty work? He didn't know the answer, but most importantly didn't want to stick around to find out.

Pushing his family in the direction of the field, Davis looked down at Pedro. "You're right, son. That building's our best option at this point. Let's get ourselves there."

And with that, the family of four took off moving once again. They pushed through the last layer of trees and emerged out into the huge grassy expanse. Davis instantly came to the full realization that what they were seeing in real time was a direct result of the large explosion that had rocked the island a short while ago. And what they saw as they continued running could only best be described as a blood-strewn nightmarish sloping grass hillside absolutely littered with bits and pieces of body parts, blood, and entrails everywhere.

All around them the grass was flattened and pressed down, great big streaks of blood everywhere and the smell, the smell itself was almost unbearable. As they ran, Davis found it literally impossible not to take it all in. Looking like something out of a war movie, body parts were strewn about everywhere. Many of the massive and formidable body parts only served to further emphasize just how large and commanding these creatures truly were.

Crossing the dead center of the field, they moved about on wet, muddy grass. They were heading toward the thick stand of trees on the far side of the huge grassy expanse.

Davis knew that once they got to the far side of the clearing and entered the trees, they'd need to make a hard left and begin hiking their way back up the steep hillside.

"Grab the kids," Davis heard a frantic voice shout out from somewhere back in the middle of the field.

A quick glance back and Davis could see that two speedy males had pulled to within about a hundred feet of them. Quickly Davis reached down and swooped Pedro off the ground. With his young son now in his arms, he sped ahead and did the same to Ariana.

"C'mon," he shouted to Elena, holding both kids in his arms. "We got company."

"Oh my God," Elena responded. There was true terror in her voice now.

Davis knew that if they could just get themselves to the top of this small track of forest, then they should be able to go right over the part of the forest on top of the Yerba Buena Tunnel that would put them on the other side of the island.

Davis and the kids plunged headfirst through the start of the trees. Making a sharp left, immediately they began ascending the steep hillside. While the grass clearing had been a soggy and at times muddy mess, they found the hillside to be rather dry and firm. But it wasn't without its own set of obstacles though. The stripped and slippery bark of the eucalyptus trees that dominated this small island littered the ground. It was going to be a treacherous and dangerous ascent up the hill.

"Watch your step," Davis yelled out to Elena.

"I can carry Ariana if needed," she fired back.

"Just keep up," Davis said plowing his way in great, powerful strides up the hillside.

Davis and Elena had managed to work their way a good forty to fifty feet up the hillside when they finally heard twigs breaking and cracking from somewhere down below them.

"There they are," someone yelled.

"Don't look back," Davis shouted. "Just keep movin'."

As they continued climbing up the hillside, Davis knew they needed to figure something out quickly. He wasn't certain how many people had taken the religious woman up on her crazed words and were now coming for their kids.

Davis believed Pedro's plan was actually the best option that they had at the moment. It was really their only option at this point.

The hillside started to become steeper as Elena climbed just a yard or so to his right. Meanwhile, from a short distance back down the hill, they heard feet sliding and slipping. To Davis it honestly felt like the weight of the world was bearing down on him. The survival of his small family of four was seated squarely atop his shoulders, literally as well as figuratively. But he just kept focusing all his power on taking it one step at a time, working closer and closer toward their end goal. Just like he had done time and time again back in his football playing days when coach would have them run conditioning drills and it was well over a hundred degrees outside. One play at a time, one down at a time, one drill at a time. If they could just get to the top of the—

A deep and cavernous roar burst forth out of nowhere, catching them all completely off guard.

"Oh God," Davis mumbled under his breath.

They continued climbing as the sound of something big moving in and about through the trees drew nearer. Scrambling their way up the last of the hillside, it was hard not to process and make out all the madness ensuing from just a short distance below them.

"Holy shit," a voice shouted out from somewhere back down the hillside.

"Hey, watch out! It's right behind—"

The voice cut off abruptly, followed by a sickening crunching sound. There was another short-lived scream from deep within the beast's jaw, followed by one last final *crunch*. What ensued next was a steady cacophony of rising voices as a wave of panic quickly overtook the hillside.

"Watch out, it's comin' in on your right."

"Hey, hey, hey."

Big monstrous steps rang out from some unseen vantage point in and amongst the trees as people continued scrambling up the hillside, trying to gain traction any way they could, trying to escape the jaws of death that had literally just come out of nowhere and already claimed one of their own.

It was difficult at this point for Davis to assess just how dedicated and committed the small crowd's full intentions were. Were they really here to carry out the crazy religious woman's wishes? Hard to tell. But the fact that it had even gotten this far to the point where he and his family were being pursued up a remote hillside told him all he needed to know.

But those that did find themselves pursuing Davis and his family up the steep hillside soon came to the realization that here on this small island in the middle of the San Francisco Bay, man and woman had been pushed down a notch on the food chain. And as another unearthly roar rang out, the reality of just where they were on that food chain came full circle.

Davis and Elena had no choice but to let all the chaos and noise filter and fade off into the background as they continued to scramble their way to the top of the hillside. That's all that mattered at this point.

Fighting off the excruciating burn in his arms, legs, as well as that of his lower back, Davis eyed the top of the hill. They were almost there. He also knew that they were still being actively pursued. But by how many people remained a mystery. They couldn't afford the time necessary to have a look back at this point.

Already, Davis was busy trying to think two steps ahead, trying to hash out his plan of attack. If they could just get themselves to this building that was currently under construction, he could push Elena and the kids into a safe hiding area and he could confront this angry and potentially dangerous mob on his own. And then it would be one against many, but at that point Davis would simply let the rage flow, let the extreme aggression that was always there, always coursing through his bloodstream, and let it out for all the world to see and experience. Throughout his whole marriage to Elena, the rage and aggression had been something he had worked on controlling, worked on getting to an acceptable and safe level. But if it did indeed come to the grim reality of him having to confront a bunch of crazed people on his own, then it would be time once and for all to let loose with everything he had. At that point there would be no holding back.

To Davis, it appeared at first glance as though no one in the angry mob behind them was armed. If there was someone that was indeed armed, they would have already been fired at. They had that much going for them at least, if that was indeed the case. The one thing that scared Davis more than anything in this world was that of gun violence. Confronting an angry mob who didn't have any unfair advantages was just fine by him. Confronting someone with a gun or a high-powered assault rifle was an entirely different issue.

Finally, at long last, Davis and Elena spilled out of the forest and came across a small road that led up at a slight angle. They ran full speed up the road. On the left of them and perched on a small hill lay another old looking white home. As expected, all the windows and front doors were boarded over solid with wood. It was indicative of society and the world at large. People had gone deep into isolation, and it was now a free for all, everyone for themselves.

"There it is, Dad," Pedro blurted out, pointing to another small track of forest that grew on the top of the tunnel that cut through the Bay Bridge, connecting one part of the island to the next.

That's where they needed to get to now. That's the route that hopefully would allow them to get safely to the other side of the bridge, but most importantly to try and get to the top of the building currently under construction. That was the plan.

The four of them had just crossed to the other side of the small road and begun climbing the next forested hillside which grew on top of the bridge tunnel when their ears were greeted with the crashing noise of those still in pursuit. And beyond the noise of feet running, Davis heard loud booming monstrous steps pursuing those that were running.

With both kids still firmly in his arms, Davis and Elena plunged headfirst back into the trees and began ascending the next steep hillside.

21

Matt Baker and Hope had finally gotten themselves to the other side of the bridge, via the small forest that grew high atop the Yerba Buena Bay Bridge tunnel. Moving quickly now, they found the large multi-story, cream-colored cement building to be just as Matt had hoped. Unfinished and currently abandoned, the only question that remained was could they find their way in? A good portion of the building was covered over and tarped in certain spots.

Hope moved alongside Matt as they ran. As they hurried their way toward the building, his eyes scanned frantically for an opening inside, anywhere.

As they ran, he finally spotted something.

On the far-left corner of the multi-storied building, Matt spotted what he had hoped would be there all along. An entrance with no door appeared to make its way back and into the building. Matt and Hope pushed themselves faster now, the dog barking loudly as they ran.

"C'mon girl," Matt shouted out to Hope, although the words were more encouragement for himself rather than his new friend at this point.

Finally reaching the opening that led into the side of the building, Matt and Hope entered through it and disappeared.

***

The enormous young predator passed by dozens and dozens of cars with its great huge strides. It moved its enormous bulk in the direction of the cyclone fence. Letting out another ungodly cry, the fifty-foot-long creature neared to within a dozen or so feet of the cyclone fence that separated the bridge itself from one part of Yerba Buena Island, more specifically a part of the island where a new high-rise building was quickly being constructed.

The huge head and the two large eyes stared in the direction of where the creature that walked upright on two legs along with the barking shaggy creature on four limbs had disappeared off to. That's where its sole attention was right now. Finally, having reached the fence, the head of the animal towered more than ten feet above the top of the fence. If it wanted too, it could use one of its huge feet to topple the pitiful fence down. Suddenly it heard noise. The noise sounded like it was coming from somewhere above it. The big head swung upward and stared in that direction.

***

Finally, having succumbed to the intense burning sensation in both his arms, legs, as well as his lower back, Davis Brown set Ariana and Pedro down on the ground. Now the family of four was once again scrambling through the trees for what seemed like the millionth time today. Davis was holding Pedro's hand, Elena holding Ariana's.

They passed through another dense patch of forest before finally catching another break in the trees. They were now on the part of the trees and forest that grew above the Yerba Buena Tunnel on the bridge. Just to their right probably a good thirty to forty feet below them lay the San Francisco-Oakland Bay Bridge. They were traversing the steep sloping hillside atop the tunnel. And then Davis noticed something. He saw one of the creatures standing just in front of the cyclone fence that stood a short distance away from the new building under construction.

He locked eyes with the young carnivore for a moment. Having suddenly spotted the four fleeing humans, Davis watched as the huge creature lurched forward several feet. They were simply too high up at this point though for the carnivore to reach them. Still eyeing the family as they navigated their way through the forest atop the tunnel, the giant creature let out a bellowing roar.

Davis also heard noise from behind them as well. It was the sound of branches and vegetation cracking and breaking, but more importantly it was the sound of them still being pursued by the small group of people. A small gathering of people who at first glance appeared hell bent on carrying out the dirty work of the religious woman, a self-proclaimed religious nut who claimed to be a warrior of God.

Davis shot another quick glance back down below them onto the bridge. The creature was still standing there staring up at them, the thick and muscular neck pointing the big head in their direction, the powerful tail stretched out behind the enormous body. Despite the young creature's overwhelming size, there was no way in hell it could get to them. They were simply too high up to reach. But the creature below them was not their immediate problem. More noise ringing out from behind them reminded Davis as to their current plight. They heard branches cracking and breaking. The group of people was quickly closing the gap on them.

"It's just up ahead, Dad," Pedro called out. "Just up ahead."

Davis and his family were now heading downward at a steep angle. This small, forested hillside atop the tunnel on the San Francisco-Oakland Bay Bridge was about to put them on the other side of the bridge. The correct side they needed to be on if they were to look for the possibility of taking refuge within the building. After that, it would be all bets off whether the building would offer up the possibility of safety.

Davis shot one last glare down toward the huge beast below them. The big head and the unwavering eyes had followed every bit of their progress through the trees atop the tunnel. Davis knew it would only be a matter of time before—

Immediately, the creature's head shot toward the family as they progressed further down the slope. They got back onto solid ground and came upon a small road. The multi-leveled building currently under construction was only a hundred feet or so away now just at the bottom of the road. Davis couldn't help but turn himself to the right. As he did so, his eyes took in the small cyclone fence that separated them from the bridge, but most importantly from the huge creature standing just on the other side of it. Now that they weren't navigating their way through the forest atop the tunnel, the only thing separating them now from this creature was a thin, flimsy cyclone fence.

The predator, upon seeing the fleeing family, took off immediately as it strode forward toward the fence.

There was nothing Davis and his family could do at this point except continue moving in the direction of the building. With the huge creature threatening to literally topple the pitifully small cyclone fence over at any given second, the rush of people coming down the sloping hillside behind them also rang loud and clear. Now Davis and his family had no choice but to push onward toward the building.

***

Pearson and Gonzalez emerged from the trees at the very top of the hillside and stepped out onto a steep road that led downward. Pearson, still gnawing on and working his wet cigar aggressively back and forth in his mouth, eyed the very bottom of the road now. Probably a good two to three hundred feet away and at the bottom of the road lay the multi-level building currently under construction. And to the right of that stood the long cyclone fence that bordered the bridge. Pearson's eyes focused in on the small family of four moving swiftly down the road toward the building.

He felt his body lurch forward on him, his big gun pressed out in front of him, literally felt the words and orders that he would shout to the family at the tip of his tongue. But no words ever left his mouth. Suddenly and with no warning whatsoever, a huge disturbance of limbs and branches exploded to life behind them. A giant mass of muscle and scales emerged out into the open.

Striding triumphantly from the trees and stretching out to its full length, the creature lowered its head and blared a deafening roar. To have been in such close proximity to the enormous, cavernous sound was a terrifying thing indeed to witness first hand, like hearing ten male lions roaring all at once on the plains of the Serengeti in Africa.

The massive predator came at them so fast and with such speed, that Pearson barely had time to even spin around and level his gun out in front of him. He managed to fire off several rounds into the thick hide of the creature as it strode forward. Pearson watched in absolute horror though, as the massive jaws opened ridiculously wide and closed down around Gonzalez.

There was a harrowing cry followed by a short-lived struggle as the jaws clamped shut around Gonzalez, ripping him off the ground, sweeping him up and into the air as if he weighed but a mere fraction of his true weight. One more wet, gurgled, shrill cry of terror rang out. From inside the great jaws lined with rows of teeth, the cry cut off abruptly. What followed next was the sound of the huge teeth chomping down on him. Blood shot out on both sides of the jaws in one final sickening display.

Pearson, having just witnessed the last one of his men meet their end, managed to get off several more shots into the enraged beast before finally abandoning his post altogether. He turned quickly and immediately began sprinting down the road. As he ran, his eyes started to take it all in, quickly assessing the evolving situation. Behind him, he could still hear the huge predator feeding on Gonzalez. The sound of bones being crushed and pulverized chilled him to the core as he ran.

A good hundred feet or so from the bottom, he saw the family of four continuing to move in the direction of the multi-leveled, tarped building. Turning to his right, Pearson both heard and saw the commotion of others.

He saw several people running in pursuit of the family of four. Or were they merely fleeing for their own lives as well? In the chaos of the moment, he simply didn't know. There was just too much going on at this point to make clear sense of things.

As Pearson neared the bottom of the road now, he eyed the charging group of people as they navigated their way down the sloping dirt hillside just to his right. And then beyond that, at the cyclone fence that bordered the bridge, Pearson eyed another one of the huge creatures. With the head of the enormous beast towering above the tiny fence, Pearson felt hesitation in his body. He felt walled in by these living monstrosities, one on the other side of the fence, the other finishing off the remains of Gonzalez at the top of the road near the start of the trees. There appeared to be no way out.

Quickly Pearson spun and eyed the man who was busy scurrying his family off in the direction of the building. He watched as the man came to a complete stop and turned himself around. And it was in that moment that Pearson saw it. The look in the man's eyes confirmed everything that Pearson needed to fully understand about the quickly evolving situation.

Pearson needed to get himself to the bottom of the small road before the scrambling crowd busy making their way down the hillside to the right reached the bottom of the road first. In an effort to get there before the others did, Pearson pushed himself into top gear now. Roaring at the top of his lungs, he did so just as the first few people made their way off the hillside and spilled out onto the open road.

And it was in that small window of time, that everything started to happen at light speed. Pearson heard more feet navigating their way down the hillside heading his way. And then beyond that his eyes locked in on the cyclone fence that bordered the bridge. He eyed the immense creature standing just on the other side of the fence, the huge predator threatening to topple it over at any second. And then, rather quickly, Pearson watched as the huge head swung in his direction.

A smoldering fire burned deep inside of Pearson now, and he could feel its warm and explosive power permeating to all parts of his body. With this new-found sense of vengeance hard on his mind, he watched as huge jaws parted ways and the predator blasted a roar. And then as he had feared all along, he watched as the big hind limb lifted high into the air and sent the huge, clawed, manhole-sized foot crashing straight down through the fence. The flimsy cyclone fence was flattened to the ground with a sickening squeal of metal being twisted and bent. It seemed pitiful, almost comical in the presence of such a commanding and powerful predator as the giant animal walked right over the fence now as though it had never even existed.

Free and no longer held back, the creature let loose a thunderous moan as it shot forward. More than twenty thousand pounds of muscle and sinew charged straight for Pearson. Meanwhile behind him, those that had officially made their way down and off the hillside had finally noticed the other charging beast further back up the road. It felt as though this had to be the true definition of hell on Earth. Yerba Buena Island had suddenly been thrust against its will into a steep decline into madness.

Pearson felt the adrenaline coursing through him now more than ever. The blood flowing to all parts of his body pumped with fury for the lives lost, for his men that had been gobbled down and slaughtered like lambs, the sheer blood loss of it all, the utter savagery. It was inhumane and not right and he was more determined now than ever to do something about it, to settle this so-called score. Pearson bit down on the cigar one last time before spitting the thing out the corner of his mouth. And then with a triumphant roar of his own, he raised his rifle above his head and charged forward.

The huge predator blasted a roar of its own as it charged straight for Pearson, covering great distances with its huge strides.

Pearson held the rifle raised above his head and screamed at the top of his lungs, charging straight for the blaring animal. Now there was only him and this magnificently constructed beast. Somewhere in the back of Pearson's brain though, deep behind the rage-filled aggression, behind the anger and utter sadness he felt for his men, there had to be a scared and terrified individual. Someone that both knew and fully understood that this was not going to end well, that this was not going to end in his favor. Certainly, he must have known this from somewhere deep inside of him. But he most definitely wasn't letting any of these fears be known by his outward appearances.

The creature let loose a thunderous cry as it strode forward on its two big legs. This prompted Pearson to unleash another terrifying cry of his own. As the commander neared to within a hundred feet of the enraged beast, he was greeted with another quick visual of just how monstrous and awe inspiringly huge these things truly were. He suddenly felt tiny and insignificant.

And it was in that moment that he truly felt the scope and insignificance of man and woman's timeline of life on this planet. The arrogance and downright hypocrisy of people to refer to something that is old and obsolete as that of a dinosaur when dinosaurs ruled this planet for some one hundred and sixty-five million years, was downright preposterous. Human's reign was going to be comically short compared to the total reign of the dinosaurs. Given the already intense rate of destruction to the planet, there simply would be no comparison, but the arrogance of humans to laugh and scoff at dinosaurs as though we were the far superior species, when, by sheer numbers of it, that couldn't have been further from the truth. This is what hit Pearson the hardest.

Pearson quickly put those thoughts behind him and prepared for battle. As he drew nearer to the charging creature, and the ground beneath his feet vibrated and shook with the intensity, he leveled his rifle out in front of him. There was no turning back now. In one quick fleeting glance, Pearson was able to do a sweep and one last final size up of the beast.

Swinging the barrel around and taking dead aim at the giant chest cavity, Pearson felt his trigger finger getting ready to press down and spray lead right into the side of the hellish beast. Charging straight at the creature now with little regard for life or limb, Pearson darted hard to his right, quickly getting himself into position for a better shot. Now with a side view of the towering creature, Pearson looked up and at the last second aimed the barrel of the rifle away from the huge chest to that of the soft underside of the neck. In a quick flash, Pearson remembered that alligators had soft spots concentrated around the face and the jaws. Perhaps such was the case with these creatures. It was certainly worth a shot.

And with that being the last credible thought that came to him, he felt his trigger finger press down as the rifle exploded to life on him. Unloading several rounds into the underside of the neck and the throat of the creature, Pearson didn't really have much time to do anything else as the huge beast countered with a devastating smack from its heavy tail.

The blow from the impact of the tail was stunning, knocking Pearson from his feet and throwing him violently through the air. It felt as though he had been struck with the trunk of a tree; the tightly coiled muscles that made up the tail was that solid and well put together. Pearson hit the ground hard on his backside, his head and back also slamming down onto the cement from the road. There was no time to catch his breath though. Knowing full well that he was now down and into a completely exposed and defenseless position forced him to his feet. As he stood and prepared to do battle, he came to the sudden realization that he was no longer in possession of his rifle.

Where the hell is it?

Quickly, he scanned his surroundings. The rifle was nowhere to be seen. With no other option in sight, Pearson reached for the large knife at his side just as the huge, gaping jaws lunged straight for him.

***

Davis put Pedro down on the ground and pushed his family in the direction of the staircase that they had all eyed at the far-left corner of the building. He watched as the three of them ran toward the stairs, the majority of the building still tarped in white to protect against the elements. Davis was just about ready to turn himself around when he saw Pedro come to a stop, turn, and stare back to him. And there for a brief yet intense second, father and son shared a tearful moment. Davis, fighting through the sudden wave of emotions, waved his son on though.

"Go," he finally shouted. "Your mom and sister need you. Watch after them."

Pedro wiped the tears from his face, turned, and sprinted off toward Elena and Ariana.

Meanwhile, Davis, fully understanding that he didn't have another second to spare, flung himself back and around prepared to fight. Rather than wait for the angry crowd to reach him, he sprinted forward in an attempt to give as much of a head start to his family as he could; put as much separation in between them and the angry worked up crowd of people as possible. The goal was to fend these lunatics off in order to give his family enough of a window to begin ascending the staircase that they had spotted only minutes prior. Hopefully this would take them to the very top of the building, or at the very least somewhere higher and safer within the building.

Davis rushed forward, ready to confront everyone and anyone who posed a threat to his family.

"There he is," someone shouted from the back of the group.

"Get 'em," another crazed voice chimed in with. "Let's run right through him."

Davis' initial thoughts were that he expected to see a much bigger gathering of people pursuing them. He had honestly expected to see everyone who had been around that enormous footprint in the mud whipped up into a frenzy by the religious woman. But what he saw instead was four. Four individuals, but four determined individuals, and most importantly four individuals that obviously weren't thinking straight, weren't processing things clearly.

The most dangerous animal is a rabid or wounded animal, Davis knew this thought to be a terrifying yet all too real reality.

And whoever these four loonies were that had taken the time to pursue them across the island this far, they were no doubt dangerous and to be treated with the upmost caution.

It was four against one. Davis had fought worse odds over the course of his life and come out victorious. But he also knew that these were far from normal times. And the fact that these were not normal times might make an individual act in a manner they might not otherwise act in. There were fires, protests, politics, the virus, and a looming financial apocalypse which threatened to topple the world at any given second. These were far from normal times and Davis knew this. He couldn't afford to overlook any of these individuals.

As Davis prepared to do battle, he could feel his whole body surging with adrenaline. The anger and aggression that he had worked so diligently to control in his family life as of late, it would soon be time to let it all out, let it come forth to the surface for all to see and experience. There would be no holding back. He needed everything he could muster and then some.

Beyond the small gathering of people, Davis saw a lone figure making its way down the hillside carefully, cautious with each step, yet working their way down the hill with a sense of purpose and determination.

"Kill the bastard," the religious woman shouted in a loud and booming voice. "Kill the bastard, then get me those two kids."

Five, Davis thought correcting his initial number. Counting the religious woman there were now five people coming straight for him. Four males and one female. But Davis didn't suspect she'd actually be a part of the fight. Obviously, she had others doing her dirty work for her.

Striding calmly and confidently, the woman navigated the last of the hillside and began to cross the road. Davis' heartrate accelerated as the religious lunatic drew nearer. He could now see that she had a rather large cross hanging prominently around her neck. The woman was now making the sign of the cross while muttering indecipherable chants to herself. It was almost as if she had gone into a trance and left her earthly body behind. It was beyond fucking unnerving.

Davis quickly focused his attention back on the small gang of people converging upon him. The group of four broke apart and fanned out wide, stalking Davis in almost the same manner as raptors would have done to their dinosaurian prey all those millions upon millions of years ago.

Davis prepared to do battle, getting himself down and into a crouched position stretching both arms wide, almost as if he was about to do a squat or play defense on someone in a basketball game. Now there was an eerie silence that had suddenly set in as the four continued closing in on him.

"Just let us take the kids and we won't hurt you," a man who probably weighed a solid two hundred and fifty pounds said, continuing to move in slowly on Davis' left side.

There was a calm and cool feeling that washed over Davis. He felt no fear, displaying not a single ounce of concern for himself. His main goal right now was to give his family as much time and head start as they could to hopefully climb their way to the very top of the building and get somewhere safe. From there the plan was to flag down one of these helicopters that they had seen circling the island from time to time. And if that wasn't a possibility at the moment, then plan B was to find somewhere to hide within the confines of the building.

Davis eyed the religious lunatic one final time. She had gotten herself to within fifty feet of the approaching group. Quickly, he noticed that she had what looked to be the holy bible out in front of her. The large gold cross that had once hung prominently around her neck was now draped across the leather-bound bible. There was also a very disturbing manner in the way in which she walked now, almost as if she was floating rather than walking, like a ghost moving silently through a graveyard. With the gold cross draped over the bible, she began speaking as if she were a priest preaching to a congregation full of the damned.

"Let it be," she said in a loud and authoritative tone. "This is God's will. Do not resist. Just let it be."

With outstretched hands, she reached out to Davis now, literally staring a hole through him in the process as her four disciples were still spread out wide and converging on him from all sides.

Davis focused his sole attention back on the small group of people closing in on him. He remained still though; his legs crouched low into a squat position with both arms spread wide. It felt like he was literally playing defense against the approaching crowd, not allowing them to pass through. He was centered and even though he was outnumbered, he felt good, felt strong, felt like the immovable object he had always been back in his collegiate football playing days. He knew that the adrenaline coursing through his body would allow him to prevail.

"Ya can't stop us," a man coming in slowly on his right said. "Ya can't stop us."

There was no reply from Davis though. He remained firm right where he was, an almost impenetrable wall of both muscle and mass as all two hundred and twenty pounds of him stood tight and coiled like a big cat ready to pounce at any moment. Despite his calm and placid outward demeanor though, the tightened and constricted muscles in Davis twitching with anticipation, awaiting the moment where he would burst to life. It was almost as if his muscles and body yearned to hit someone again. To get that intoxicating feeling and sensation of knocking someone flat on their ass. And it couldn't have come at a better time.

Still eyeing the approaching four, Davis spread his hands and arms out as far and wide as they could go now. He prepared for battle while maintaining visual on all four of them. From somewhere behind the approaching group, the woman's voice could still be heard.

"It is God's will," she said in very low and almost theatrical tone. "And who are we as mere mortals to interfere with the will of God?"

Davis watched as she pointed her face to the sky, lifting both the bible and dangling cross up with it as well. "Lord, if this is truly your will, then I as your humble servant shall ensure that it gets done. It shall be done. Just as your words and will were inscribed in the good book I hold in these hands, your will shall be done here on Earth. It shall be done. It shall be done."

The woman with her neck and head still tilted toward the sky, drew in several deep breaths. And then with a quick burst she slammed the bible shut, lowered her head, and set her gaze squarely on Davis. Her monotone words came fast and hard now.

"Kill all those that stand in the way of these necessary sacrifices," she said.

Meanwhile, Davis watched as the group, seeming to be as if they were under the hypnotic trance of the woman, finally came to life. A man on his left shot forward, arms outstretched, coming at him as though he was going to tackle him to the ground as if it were a football game.

As the man burst forward, Davis had time to quickly size him up. The man was more or less the same size as him, give or a take a few pounds here and there. But he was nowhere near the physical specimen that Davis was. Charging hard like a bull, no further thought could be put into this as the man came at Davis with a good deal of speed.

Davis took two steps forward. In one coordinated move, he lowered his center of gravity, lunged for the man's mid-section, and tossed him up and over his head. Davis Brown manhandled the man as though he weighed a mere fraction of what he actually did.

Davis couldn't afford to pay any more attention to the original attacker as the others came at him. But from just a few feet behind him, he could hear the sickening thud of the man whom he tossed into the air finally hit the ground hard.

The next attacker was much smaller, but a fit, strong man, nonetheless. Davis rushed out to greet the man. He grabbed the fucker by both shoulders and threw him hard to the ground. The man hit the ground hard on his backside. The stunning impact of the man's head striking the ground instantly drew blood from the back of his cracked skull. Immediately he began writhing in pain on the ground while clutching the back of his head.

Davis felt the surging rage coursing through his bloodstream like a drug hard at work. Completely enraged, it was as if he was back playing college football once again, all his frustrations, all his anger at not passing the bar, never having been able to get a small business up and running successfully—everything that had happened to him over the course of his life, it was all fueling the rage like one great big-towering inferno. And now he was wielding that very rage and aggression as though it were a lifeline that had just been given to him.

"Who wants some?" Davis roared at the top of his lungs. "Who the fuck wants some? Who's next?"

He turned and swiveled as he faced the remaining attackers.

"Ah, violence and aggression," the religious woman said from somewhere close by. "It has been the plight of mankind since what seems like the dawn of time. And it has never been a good strategy to employ and implement."

The two men that Davis had knocked and sent to the ground were still down. If for some reason or another they did manage to get up and stagger to their feet, Davis fully intended on reminding them where they belonged.

It was also in that moment that he realized that his family couldn't run forever, and that if they were to truly have the time needed to flag down help from high above, then he one hundred percent needed to disable and immobilize every last one of these individuals that had come in pursuit of them. Davis had every intention of immobilizing each of them to the point where walking was no longer an option.

From somewhere close by, the religious woman continued to preach. "While your bravery and heroism will no doubt go down as being remembered here today, make no doubt about it, we will get what we came for."

Davis backed himself up several feet, his legs still spread wide in a powerful squat position, his arms still fully extended. He stood there like a wall, built like a mini tank, as the adrenaline continued surging through him. Nothing in this world was going to get by him. He needed to defend his family. This was the reality of the ever-evolving situation that he suddenly found himself thrust into. There was no running from this, it needed to be confronted head on.

He watched as the other two men, each who had to outweigh him by a good hundred pounds or so continued advancing forward. Despite their enormous size advantage over him, they moved forward with caution.

"This is not gonna end well for whoever's left," Davis announced. "Let's just put this to rest and no one else needs to get hurt. Deal?"

From behind the two huge men, the religious woman laughed, almost scoffing at the statement. Her words once again came quick and fast. "Kill him. Now. Then get the children."

22

Commander Gray Pearson had just managed to unsheathe the large Ka-Bar knife at his side when suddenly a colossal set of jaws bigger than a bathtub clamped down around his waist and closed shut. Dagger-like teeth from the top and bottom part of the massive creature's jaws bit down around his legs and waist, instantly sweeping Pearson up and off the ground and lifting him high into the air.

Pearson felt the sudden rush of air as he was lifted higher and higher. Somehow though, he managed to maintain his grip on the knife. Out of options and pinned tightly in place between the rows of huge teeth, he drew the Ka-Bar knife back as far as he could and stabbed at the great beast somewhere along the lower part of the jaw. The impact of the tip of the knife to the creature's skull appeared futile at this point. The huge beast seemed to hardly even notice the pitiful human weapon as it bounced off the thick hide and dense bone that lay beneath.

Pearson once again stabbed at the lower jaw. Again, the act itself seemed futile and pointless against such a monstrosity. Suddenly though, the animal released its jaws just enough for Pearson to wiggle free and change his positioning in and amongst the fierce rows of teeth. When the jaws finally closed tightly once again around him, Pearson all of a sudden found himself close to the one of the huge eyeballs.

He stared at the huge unwavering eye for a fleeting second, saw the giant baseball sized eye twitching in the socket. And then in a flash, Pearson drew the knife back in his right hand and sent it plunging full force straight into the great eye. Pearson forced the knife into the eye as far as it would go. With the knife now protruding out of the huge eye socket, having been plunged all the way to the hilt, the creature screamed a piercing shrill cry, the sound itself rumbling from the great chest cavity. The animal threw its head back and forth to both sides in sharp protest.

The knife to the giant eyeball had done just as Pearson hoped it would. He felt the great jaws suddenly open just enough to release him. Wasting no time, he pushed off, wiggled himself free, and fell toward the ground.

Pearson's fall from the massive jaws some fifteen feet above the ground had been anything but graceful. He hit the dirt hard and instantly rolled onto his side into a tightly formed ball. As soon as he was able to stagger to his feet, Pearson began moving out and away from the towering creature still thrashing its head and neck back wildly above him. The pain from the driving knife had momentarily sent the huge animal into a world of blinding, searing pain.

Quickly, Pearson worked on getting his bearings straight. He desperately needed to locate his rifle. But things were happening too fast at this point for his eyes to in fact process the exact whereabouts of the weapon. He spun around just as he watched the huge creature turn its head around and watch the man out of its good eye.

Pearson caught sight of the knife handle still protruding out of the carnivore's right eye socket. With the way in which the creature had its head cocked to one side, Pearson suspected that he had blinded the beast in its right eye.

As the gaping jaws parted ways, a low rumbling bellowing sound emanated from the creature's cavernous maw. Pearson knew better, though, than to think that his brazen attack on the predator's eyeball had and could stop such a large and determined animal. If anything, he had simply just further enraged it. When the creature suddenly lowered its head and stretched its neck out to its full length while letting out a deep, moaning roar, Pearson's fears were confirmed.

He watched as the gargantuan, horned predator lurched forward and took off in pursuit of him. Lowering its head and charging, it appeared as though the animal wanted to gore him to death with its horns. Pearson was momentarily caught off guard by the tidal wave of repressed energy steamrolling his way. And it was hard not to stare, hard not to be a literal deer in the headlights when something so large was moving that fast. The feeling of the ground vibrating beneath his boots sprung him back to life as the creature let loose a throaty, moaning roar.

Pearson finally caught sight of his rifle. It was laying down on the ground somewhere off to his right. The question was could he get to it in time? For a brief second, he thought he couldn't reach it, that he simply couldn't get there in time before the creature got to him. But he desperately needed to get the weapon back, needed to have all that firepower once again at his fingertips.

Pearson took off at a dead sprint. Quickly, he got his body up to speed, his eyes focusing in on one thing and one thing only: his rifle. He needed to get it back at all costs. Sprinting at top speed, he fully understood the consequences of going after the rifle like this. It just may cost him his life. Not allowing himself to take his eyes off the rifle, he was still able to see the giant predator tracking him down out of the corner of his left eye. But he forced himself not to stretch the view any further than that. He was almost to the rifle now.

He could smell the pungent stench of the animal, and it was the thick smell alone that made him think the creature was in fact closer than it actually was. But Pearson had also underestimated his own footspeed, not given himself enough credit. Lowering his right hand, he reached down and swooped the rifle off the ground. It was an exhilarating feeling to once again be back in possession of the weapon. He didn't have a moment to spare though. Without stopping all his forward-moving momentum, he allowed himself a split second to check on where the creature was in relation to him. He saw the massive, clawed, manhole-sized feet crashing down with each huge stride the giant animal took. Pearson pushed off with both legs and immediately sent himself in the opposite direction. For a second, it was difficult to get his body back up to speed. Holding the rifle in his right hand, he pumped his arms and legs for all they were worth as he let out a scream. Pure survival and adrenaline was all that powered him forward at this point.

And with that, Commander Gray Pearson fled back toward the small gathering of people just a short distance up the road.

23

Davis heard the creature pursuing the military man back up the road headed their way. But there was nothing he could do at this point except focus his attention solely on the two huge men converging upon him. He had gone into a hyper awareness mode, his body absolutely surging with survival adrenaline.

"Let's call this shit off," Davis shouted to the two approaching men, his arms still spread wide in a defensive posture. "This is crazy. We don't have to do this."

"Hey, fuck you, pal," one of them replied in a low booming voice. "World's gone to shit. We're all fucked."

Davis glared at the man while also eyeing the other approaching man. And then for a brief second, he shifted his attention beyond the two approaching men. He could see the military man running in their direction, and just a short distance behind him Davis could see what was aggressively pursuing him.

When Davis returned his eyes toward the two approaching men, the attack officially began. The two of them came at him with surprising speed. And it was in that split second that Davis could see just what type of fight he was in for. Given the size that both men possessed, they moved with considerable speed.

Davis, having to make a quick decision which man to go for, threw his body toward the man on the far left at the very last second. All two hundred and twenty pounds of Davis Brown struck the man with everything he had. The man, easily outweighing Davis by a good hundred pounds, took the blow as though he were an immovable object. To Davis it felt as though he had crashed head-first straight into a brick wall.

Davis wasted no time, though, as he rattled off a quick succession of swift punches to the man's gut. His punches struck with such force that it momentarily caused the man to stumble backward. But no sooner had the man stumbled backward when Davis was hit hard from behind. The fierce blow to his back knocked him to the ground. As Davis fell forward, he could see the original man whom he had struck in the gut rushing forward as well.

Down on the ground and defenseless, Davis knew he was out of options. Davis had just gotten himself off the ground and into a crouched position when he struck the original attacker in the genitals. He threw that punch to the man's privates with every last ounce of strength he had. At this point Davis felt no shame for what he had done. It was kill or be killed, and at this juncture of the game, anything and everything was fair game. There were no rules at this point.

As Davis watched the man crumble to his knees in agonizing pain, he was suddenly attacked from behind. He felt huge arms wrap around his neck and before he could do anything else, he found himself being strangled. The man at his back was overwhelmingly powerful. Davis roared at the top of his lungs as his airwaves were slowly being cut off, choking him to death. The man at his back was also trying to force Davis to his knees, perhaps thinking that if he was down laying on his stomach, he'd be an easier kill, easier to finish off.

Struggling to breathe Davis felt dizzy, desperately in need of a huge fulfilling breath of air. He struggled to get another breath in, but felt the huge arms around his neck tighten even further like an anaconda slowly squeezing its prey to death.

He needed to do something, and fast. Visions of his family quickly flashed in his brain like quick moving images and shots in a movie. His saw his life, his past, present and future endeavors. He saw Elena. And then lastly, he saw his kids. Pedro's and Ariana's lives hinged on their dad's ability to hold these loonies off. If he succumbed to them, then it would be completely up in the air if his family ever got off this island alive. He couldn't let that happen.

Hardly able to breathe, he was almost out of air. He gathered himself and, with everything he had, sent the back of his head into the attacker still clinging tightly to him. Because the man was pressed up so tightly against Davis leaving little to no room in between the two, the blow from the back of Davis' head to the man's chin did not strike with the force that Davis had hoped it would. Davis remained in the chokehold as he neared unconsciousness now. His lungs screamed for air.

While Davis' neck and airwaves had been cut off, the large man behind him failed to restrain Davis' arms. This left an opening. It was all that Davis had. Reaching back with both arms Davis latched onto the man. Years and years of squeezing tennis balls in an effort to build up both his wrists as well as his grip pressure were on full display as his outstretched fingertips sunk down and into the man with devastating force. Davis prepared his lower legs and his upper body as though he was going to do a squat with a bar. And then with everything he could muster, he lifted the huge man from behind up and over his head and body slammed him.

The back of the man splashed down into a cold muddy puddle as his back took the blow square on. Now free of the man, Davis desperately sucked in a giant breath of air. He spun around in all directions to gain a better semblance of things.

A gut-wrenching cry accompanied by an immense crunching sound suddenly assaulted Davis' ear. And then almost out of nowhere, an overwhelmingly sharp and pungent odor like rotten garbage overtook the area. Another wet, gurgled cry of terror rang out from what sounded like somewhere deep within the cavernous jaws of one of the creatures. Someone had just been killed and eaten. But who? In the madness of it all, it was difficult for Davis to take stock of who was left, to make sense of the entire situation.

Davis saw the man who he had just thrown up and over his shoulders struggling to turn himself over in the deep muddy puddle. He was not far from where Davis stood. But after that it was difficult to make sense of where everyone else had run off to. None of that was of importance though as in a matter of seconds they had all just been dropped a notch down on the food chain. Davis' attention quickly turned elsewhere. And with good reason.

A deep bellowing sound heralded the arrival of one of the creatures. Davis spun around right where he was, his attention now focused solely on a predator that represented as sure a thing as death itself. Huge jaws lined with massive teeth that possessed the ability to open at a terrifyingly wide angle. It simply was an unfair predator.

Davis watched as a chilling sight suddenly came into plain view. The religious woman materialized out of nowhere, almost as though she had emerged out of thin air itself. She held the bible still clasped in her outstretched hands with the gold chain draped across the leather cover of the book.

And then Davis heard another bellowing rumble which signaled the arrival of a second creature, this one visibly larger than the first. He watched as two of the huge monsters converged on the woman from both sides before finally bringing themselves to a stop. The woman now stood walled in between the tree-sized limbs of both carnivores. She glared back at Davis, showing very little worry or concern for her current predicament. The rain had picked back up once again and was really coming down hard now, pounding the small island as though it wanted to drown the tiny rock in the middle of the San Francisco Bay in its wrath.

The woman yelled to be heard over the rain.

"Do not fear these beasts, for it is not they that you should fear," she announced triumphantly.

She held the bible above her head now as water ran down all sides of it.

"These creatures," the woman continued, still having to yell over the onslaught of rain. "These creatures are not to be feared, rather they are to be revered. They are top apex predators, fashioned out of blood, claws, teeth, and flesh. They have been created in the same manner as the lord created humans. With the same care and painstaking attention to detail."

The woman paused for a moment, gathered herself, and stared up at one of the great beasts. From where she was positioned, she stood directly beneath the huge neck, staring up at the bottom of the cavernous jaws. Rainwater continued cascading down the huge beast's head like mini waterfalls that fell relentlessly onto the woman below.

"These creatures," the woman yelled through the rain, "are the rightful heirs to this planet, and they will inherit this mess once mankind has literally imploded on itself. Centuries upon centuries of bad mistakes compounding themselves one after the other. They will inherit all our wasteful and damaging ways and be left to deal with the aftermath of our blunders."

From somewhere off a few miles away, lightning suddenly lit up the sky in a white-hot sizzle, followed by the rumble of thunder. From where Davis was positioned and standing, it was beyond a surreal sight to see the woman nestled in between the legs of both great beasts with the bible still held high above her head. It literally felt like the end of days was upon the world.

She continued speaking. "These creatures are the rightful rulers of this planet. This world belongs to them now. Not us. And it is high time that they finally ascend and assume their rightful position at the top. We must step down as the dominant species."

As lightning continued to light up the sky and the thunder relentlessly rumbled like some type of demonic bass guitar, Davis suddenly was attacked from behind. He felt powerful arms and legs quickly overtake him. Completely entranced with the sight of the woman standing in between the two giant predators with the bible still clenched firmly in both hands, he had failed to hear the attack from behind. Now he found himself in the clutches of several of the men whom he had just dismantled. It was difficult to make sense which of the men he had fought off now held him against his will. The only thing that he knew with certainty was that he felt large and powerful hands controlling him. But most importantly, he felt those hands forcing him in the direction of the woman still walled in between the two giant animals.

**

"This way, Mom," Pedro Brown shouted from just a few stairs ahead of Ariana and his mom.

The three had thankfully managed to find an opening into the incomplete building and stairwell located at one of the far corners of the building. And they were now traversing that very stairwell right this very minute. As they ascended higher and higher up the building, they passed by floor after floor loaded with construction materials of all sorts from rebar to heavy machinery, to wires dangling and hanging everywhere. The firsthand evidence of a building still very much currently under construction.

Pedro flew up the next flight of stairs. He had always possessed good speed and been one of the fastest amongst his classmates, and now that speed was on full display as he climbed the stairs faster and faster. Meanwhile, from what appeared to be somewhere inside the building, he heard a loud bellowing sound. The deep moaning cry seemed to resonate from one floor to the next.

Could one of the creatures actually be inside the

building, Pedro thought to himself with a chill, breathing hard as a wave of panic quickly washed over him.

Obviously, there was no way that one of their huge bodies could fit inside these tight and constricting stairwells. What about the rest of the building though? Pedro rounded the flight of stairs and headed for the next level of the building. The building was quite a bit larger, with more stories than he would have guessed. But as he continued running, he found himself quite unnerved at what he had just heard. He had already seen visible evidence to suggest that these creatures could go down on all fours and potentially walk from time to time. Although it appeared as though they spent the vast majority of their time walking around on two enormous legs, the possibility at least existed that they could walk on four limbs on occasion. In this sense they reminded Pedro of Spinosaurus, an enormous sail-backed predatory dinosaur that lived in North Africa some ninety-five million years ago and would have hunted and patrolled the wide rivers that dominated that part of Africa at the time.

But these creatures were no dinosaurs that he had ever been aware of based on all the studying and research he had done on them in his eight plus years on this planet. They did however possess extremely long forelimbs which seemingly would give them the ability to walk on all fours if needed. Pedro knew that there was no way an animal standing close to twenty feet tall could stand upright in any of the levels in this building. Could one actually be inside moving about on four limbs? He didn't know the answer to that chilling question. It was almost impossible for Pedro to speculate at this point how tall these creatures would be when moving about on all fours. But even if they could go down on all fours and manage to somehow get inside the building and to fit their enormous forms on one of these floors, it seemed highly unlikely they could travel from level to level. They'd be stuck, trapped. Pedro knew that as long as they kept moving higher and higher into the building, they'd more than likely be okay. They continued doing just that.

Pedro suddenly brought himself to a complete stop. He had been running so fast that he had momentarily left both his mom and sister behind. Breathing hard, his small chest heaved in and out as he turned himself around on the stairwell. Without giving it any further thought, he quickly began making his way back down the stairs toward them.

24

The pounding rain and storm had subsided just long enough for Davis to hear the religious woman reading passages straight from the bible, still walled in on both sides by the two terrifying predators. But as the men continued pushing Davis from behind in her direction, he could hear that the woman's narration was coming off as more nervous than anything else. Perhaps she had underestimated these creatures. Perhaps she was now doubting herself entirely. Perhaps she was doubting the mission she set out to achieve given her current predicament now. Whatever the reason may have been, she now appeared slightly unsure of herself. And in her uncertainty, she had taken to reading straight from the word of God itself.

For a moment, Davis wondered to himself why the powerful individuals that had suddenly overtaken him from behind had not completely abandoned this insane cause altogether? Perhaps the giant creatures roaming this island, not to mention the building-sized monstrosity that had destroyed part of the bridge, coupled with everything else going on in the world had something to do with it. It certainly as hell seemed as though it was everyone for themselves now. Quickly, Davis' mind shot back to that of his kids and wife. He simply had to get back to them at all costs. That's all that mattered now.

And as Davis was pushed closer to the woman and the two creatures, he realized that maybe they hadn't abandoned this woman yet because she was still alive. Anyone else given her predicament would have already been traveling down their throats into their massive stomachs by now. But for some reason or another that hadn't been the case. Perhaps this simple fact that she hadn't been killed and eaten yet, kept them committed to her cause, no matter how insane by all outward appearances it was.

All of a sudden Davis locked his knees up in stern protest and wouldn't go any further. For some reason or another, his captors from behind didn't seem to mind too much as they too brought themselves to a stop as well. And there the small group remained, completely out in the open and exposed to the elements, staring up at the two huge carnivores not more than twenty-five feet away from where they stood.

"Well, well, well," the woman yelled through the rain staring up at the two monstrosities towering above her, water still dripping and cascading down their snouts. "Looks like we're all in quite a predicament now, aren't we?"

There was no response from Davis. He felt awed, humbled, and most importantly terrified to be so close to such monstrous animals. He assumed the two behind him were no doubt experiencing the same type of terror being so close to creatures so breathtakingly large and imposing.

Suddenly, the creature on the woman's left lurched forward and moved closer to her.

Davis watched as the big head lowered itself and the fearsome jaws parted ways, exposing rows of wet, glistening teeth. A deep rumbling sound emanated from the open mouth hovering a mere few feet from the woman's head.

"Well," the religious woman shouted nervously. "Our lord and creator most certainly can work in mysterious ways at times."

Davis saw that she was eying the terrifying animal out of the corner of her eye. He watched as a combination of rainwater and saliva from the lower jaw continued to drip down and onto her head.

And then suddenly the woman's head shot quickly in Davis' direction. Her eyes flared wide with lunacy, only further cementing her downward decent into madness. The whites of her eyes said everything, fueled by all the hate imaginable in the world. And that repressed anger like a tidal wave of momentum was being directed solely at Davis as she pointed the bible straight at him now. "It's him you want, not me. I'm just the humble messenger of your word, Lord. He is the non-believer, the sinner. Now get him."

The woman's words had come out roaring at the top of her lungs, almost as if in that moment she was summoning something else other than simply her own earthly voice. Davis felt himself be released from behind and pushed violently. He fell hard to the ground, splashing down in a muddy puddle of water.

Davis knew there wasn't a moment to spare as he felt the ground move under the immense weight of one of the creatures as it strode forward on two powerful legs. He was in the process of forcing himself out of the puddle and to his feet when suddenly he felt an elbow followed by a fist collide straight into his face. Davis was knocked hard from the blows to his face, falling back helplessly once again into the puddle. Everything began to happen at lightspeed now. Coming in fast and swift, he saw what appeared to be the butt of an assault rifle as it knocked one of the attackers straight in the jaw. From such a close distance Davis heard every bit the sound of the butt of the rifle as it collided with the bone of someone's skull.

Forcing himself up and out of the puddle, Davis could see that whoever this man was that had literally come out of nowhere to aid him, he was obviously highly trained and skilled. The man wielded the assault rifle with absolute precision. Davis watched a second attacker come out of nowhere charging straight for the man. The man countered with another swift blow, this time using the barrel of the rifle and delivering a devastatingly powerful hit square onto the attacker's face. Both blows from the rifle had rendered two very large men unconscious.

Wet and dripping head to toe with cold muddy water, Davis watched the man that had literally come out of nowhere to his aid. Whoever this dirty, bloody, individual dressed in army fatigues was, there was absolutely no doubt that this person was a highly trained assassin. And then from somewhere behind Davis, he heard a terrifying scream.

Davis turned and watched in horror as the huge gaping jaws of one of the creatures closed down tightly around the religious woman's head and upper half of her body. The monstrous teeth closed shut with a sickening snap and lifted her from the ground. Meanwhile, the second creature thundered forward and bit down around the lower half of her body and legs. Both creatures lifted their colossal heads up high into the air, each having their own piece of the woman before finally the body broke in two, severing somewhere around the waist with a sickening snap.

A powerful arm grabbed Davis from behind. "C'mon," Commander Gray Pearson said through gritted teeth. "That meal won't hold them for very long."

Pearson composed himself, took aim with the rifle, and unloaded several rounds, peppering both creatures with a spray of bullets on the soft underside of their necks. From such a close distance the sound of the rifle going off and suddenly exploding to life was a deafening roar to Davis. Davis spun and tried to locate the individuals that had momentarily taken him hostage. They were nowhere to be seen, and with good reason.

Pearson turned and pointed with the barrel of the smoking rifle toward the building that Davis' family had just run off to. "Let's go; it's our best chance of survival at this point."

Davis was just about to turn and follow Pearson's lead when his eyes caught sight of something through the rain. Lying in a shallow pool of muddy water, he eyed the bible. And next to it, sat the gold cross, the two objects seeming as though they could never leave one another's side, forever locked in an eternal embrace. Perhaps in her last moments on Earth the religious woman had given up entirely on her cause, lost faith herself, or perhaps it was just chance that both had not accompanied her into the great jaws of death. Whatever the reason may have been, the bible and cross remained here on Earth, while her physical body had made two separate journeys into both creature's massive stomachs. The woman was now more than likely with her maker, her creator, facing whatever hellish fate awaited her.

The sound of huge feet once again on the move broke Davis from his thoughts. And with that he turned and began running through the rain in pursuit of Pearson.

25

The two creatures took a few seconds longer to polish off their respective meals. Being hyper carnivores, they were doing just what nature intended them to do—kill, consume, and eat fresh hunks of meat. To support their accelerated growth all the way through to adulthood, they needed to feed daily. This was all in the effort to get them to be the size of a small city building; the same size that their mother was.

Meanwhile, the rain continued to pound down atop their heavily muscled backs, soaking them, the water itself running down their thick coarse hides in tiny streams everywhere. Through the heavy storm, they eyed the two men as they ran toward the large rain-soaked building. And then with several loud booming steps, the two giant predators took off in pursuit.

***

Davis Brown could both hear and feel the two giants moving behind him. With huge, powerful strides they were each closing the distance gap on him. The hard rain had quickly subsided and had now been replaced instead with a thick white mist that fell from the sky, blanketing everything in a heavy layer of white fog. Davis wasn't able to see Pearson up ahead through the dense fog, and worst of all he wasn't able to see the building that his family had just run off to either. It was a complete whiteout to say the least. Visibility was only a few feet at best and Davis could only see his outstretched hands in front of him as he ran. He had seen these types of bleak and dismal conditions before having grown up in the Bay Area, the type of thick fog that could take a normal freeway such as Highway 1 out by the Pacific Ocean and turn it into one long continuous stretch where visibility would be reduced to only several feet or so in front of one's headlights. It was this type of all-encompassing fog that seemed to have now completely overtaken the entire island. And it had all happened in a relatively short period of time. It was very representative of typical San Francisco weather, utterly unpredictable at any time of day.

Oh shit, Davis thought, suddenly bringing himself to a complete stop and turning his body around in confusion.

In the madness and disorientation of it all, coupled with the fact that the heavy fog had literally blown in out of nowhere, Davis had gotten himself momentarily turned around. He could hear the two predators still moving about out there somewhere in the fog. They were close by. He could smell them. But he couldn't tell exactly just where they were. He couldn't tell where anything was for that matter.

Fuck.

The two animals were very close now. His heart was pounding. Davis remained frozen right where he was, enshrouded on all sides by thick walls of fog. He heard a deep snorting sound followed by a low guttural grunt. The sound reminded him of seeing the huge and intimidating walruses when he would visit the city zoo back when he was a kid. But now as he stood there in the fog completely out in the open and exposed, the sounds of breathing and air shuddering in and out of the huge chest cavities was utterly terrifying. All it would take was a sudden gust of wind to momentarily blow a thick pocket of fog aside, and he would be completely exposed. If that indeed happened, he'd be a goner. End of story for certain.

Davis forced the air as quietly in and out as he could now. More deep, rumbling breathing could be heard from close by. A gentle gust of wind brought with it a wave of awful stench. He could hear the creature's huge limbs and feet moving; knew the damn thing was close simply by the horrific smell that had now completely overtaken the area. Davis heard more air shuddering in and out of a giant chest cavity. It was utterly terrifying to be so close to these things.

For a moment, time itself seemed to stand still for Davis as he just stood there, frozen in place, breathing quietly. Everything had fallen deafly silent. Somewhere in the far reaches of his brain, behind the survival adrenaline currently coursing through his veins, he wondered if they could smell him too. Was he upwind or downwind? He didn't know.

Straining with both ears now to make sense of the white void he had suddenly been thrust into; his ears picked up on some noise. It appeared to be coming from behind. Quickly he turned himself around with the full realization that he had been blindsided.

He watched as a hand suddenly emerged through the fog reaching for him.

"Told you to stay close," Pearson whispered in a growl.

Davis instantly took hold of Pearson's hand just as a monstrous shape emerged through the fog at their backs. Davis was pulled through the fog by Pearson, and together the two took off running toward the building. One of the creatures was now not more than a dozen feet or so behind, crashing toward them with great huge strides.

***

"It's just right up ahead, Mom," Pedro Brown said, doing his best to put on a brave face, but all he could honestly think of at this point was the safety and well-being of his dad. He couldn't stop thinking about him. Was he okay? Was he injured and in need of help? Had the crowd of people overtaken him? Or had he already suffered a far worse fate?

Enough. Pedro shook his head to himself, trying to shake off that last thought.

The three of them flew up the last flight of stairs. Pedro could feel that they were close now as cold wind blew down the stairwell. Just up ahead, he could see light streaming down those first few stairs, illuminating the final steps that would take them outside. Blowing in like something out of a horror movie, he could see what looked like a combination of fog and thick drizzle. Pedro knew this was just what they had been hoping for. This stairwell would take them to the roof. From there they would at least be high off the ground and hopefully protected. But what about all this thick and dense fog? If they were truly as heavily socked in with fog as Pedro believed them to be, then that meant that no one would be able to see the roof, but more importantly not able to signal to help for any helicopters that might be circling high in the sky. This was potentially a very big problem.

With this growing concern firmly etched in the back of his mind now, they ascended the last few stairs before finally emerging out into the light. As they left the cold and dark cement stairwell behind, they were instantly engulfed in a thick gray fog. The whiteout conditions were so dismal that it took them all a moment for them to get their bearings straight. They were on top of the building in what could best be described as some type of future outside eating area and place to lounge by what more than likely would be a heated pool. The building had that type of high-end luxury feel to it.

"There," Pedro shouted pointing.

The three of them took off moving carefully across the roof of the building now. The thick pockets of fog had thinned just enough on account of the wind to reveal that they weren't alone on this rooftop. They were others, others that had had the same idea as themselves, and that was to get safely to the highest point on the island where they could hopefully wave to someone for help. Sounded simple enough, but nothing in this life ever was.

They watched and ran toward the small group of people waving their arms back and forth trying to get the attention of any helicopters that might have been passing by overhead. As the three of them approached the tiny gathering of people, Pedro could see by a quick headcount that there had to be about six or seven of them, each waving their hands in the air frantically, each hoping for a momentary break in the thick cloud cover above to reveal their desperate attempt to be rescued from this hellish nightmare.

As Pedro, Ariana, and Elena arrived next to the gathering of people, quick nods of the heads were exchanged but not much other than that. Instantly, Elena and her two kids joined in with the others, waving their arms back and forth for anyone to see. Anyone at all who might be up there in the sky. No one shouted or made any audible sounds for fear of being heard down below on the ground.

Somewhere out there high above them, covered behind the dense veil of clouds, fog, and mist, they could hear the faint rotors of a helicopter thumping. This was their chance.

Everyone continued waving their arms back and forth, trying desperately to be spotted. Quietly and unassumingly though, Pedro Brown took a few unnoticed steps away from the group. He waited and listened intently with his ears.

He felt a sinking feeling of hopelessness with the quick realization that the sound of the rotors seemed to be heading out and away from them, permanently covered behind the fog as though it were a blanket of white.

Damn, he cursed silently to himself.

The mere act of the swear word itself brought him to a swift halt. He knew he would have received quite a mouthful and a stern talking to regarding the use of the word from his dad. His dad would have really torn him a new one for using the word *damn.*

Dad, Pedro thought to himself. *Gotta get him back; make sure he's okay.*

Pedro took one last look back to the group, his eyes focusing in on his mom and sister. And then, he slipped away unnoticed.

***

Pushing full steam ahead now through the thick passages of fog still blanketing the ground, Davis Brown was running for his very existence, pushing with every last fiber of his being to get to the building before they reached him. He could both hear and feel the two creatures behind him in their frenzied pursuit to get to them. To rip them to shreds, pulls their bones apart limb from limb, and send them both to an untimely death at the very bottoms of their enormous stomachs. It felt as though the entire world around Davis was shaking and everything was converging upon him. It seemed as though the world wanted to end him.

Davis smelled the awful rotten odor that was close on his heels. The pungent aroma produced by the two huge carnivores together reeked like a hundred feasting lions on the plains of the Serengeti of Africa.

Davis continued running not only for his life, but for his family's life as well, hoping and praying that the building would materialize out of the fog before both of them met their untimely demise.

***

If Pedro Brown's decision had been met with any doubt by his own eight-year-old brain, surely the deep cavernous roars from somewhere down at ground level had only served as reassurance that he was doing the right thing, had made the correct decision to abandon his mom and sister along with the small gathering of people atop the roof in pursuit of his dad.

He ran hard down the darkened stairwell now, careful not to get tripped up on the steps when again he heard another moaning cry from somewhere down at ground level. The monstrous blast resonated and echoed all the way up the stairwell. Despite the innate terror coursing through his small body, he kept carefully making his way down the stairs. His dad's life was potentially in danger, and he knew there wasn't a moment to spare.

***

The realization that Davis wasn't going to make it to the building in time hit him full on as the creature bore down on him from behind with huge strides. With the full acceptance that he was more than likely about to be eaten alive, Davis didn't give up though, he wouldn't let himself. He kept moving swiftly in the intended direction of the building. While keeping his speed up, he managed to turn himself around ever so slightly to have a look behind him. The thick fog had dissipated just enough to allow him to see the big head and the long, oversized front limbs tipped with massive razor-sharp claws push just ahead through the fog.

The horrific sight of the front portion of the creature's lethal weaponry spurred Davis on now. The towering creature let loose a thunderous cry from just yards behind him. Davis could feel the sickening panting hot breath practically upon the hairs of his neck. The thing was literally right behind him now. It was almost all over.

***

Pedro flew down the last flight of stairs and emerged out into the thick gray fog. Quickly trying to get his bearings straight, he could see that the all-encompassing fog had now been reduced to thick pockets of scattered fog here and there. It offered him a brief yet horrifying glimpse into what was going on down at ground level here.

And then suddenly from somewhere out there in one of the dense pockets of fog, he heard noise. He took off running in the direction of the new yet surprisingly familiar sound.

Sprinting full speed, Pedro shot straight through a thick pocket of fog before emerging out on the other side. He darted hard to his right in pursuit of the barking dog. He wasn't certain how long the barking dog had been running around down here yapping up a storm. But just where in the hell was it? Even if he could get a hold of it, could he get to it in time to use it distract the giant rampaging beast?

The dog let out a few more loud yapping cries. Pedro changed directions quickly, this time darting hard to his left. It sounded as though the dog was close now. Just around and through the next thick pocket of—

Pedro literally slammed right into the barking furry animal. He seemed to be as startled by the dog's sudden appearance as it was to him. Pedro immediately bent down to pick the dog up, but the dog weighed too much and had worked itself up into quite a fury to be controlled in such a manner at this point. Pedro had just managed to get hold of the dog's collar when suddenly it bolted free of him, slipping right on by his outstretched fingers.

He was certain that his mistake would cause the dog to dart off and disappear. But to Pedro's surprise, the dog had only gone off a few yards or so before quickly returning. Perhaps it was confused down here, or simply just scared out of its mind, or possibly both. Whatever the reason might have been, it continued barking loudly for all it was worth. It's yapping cries through the fog hadn't gone unnoticed though.

Whether out of sheer terror or simply the sight of seeing something so breathtakingly enormous suddenly stomping his way, young Pedro Brown took off running. He wasn't certain where he was headed, just that he couldn't afford to stick around. He didn't fancy ending up at the bottom of one of these beasts' enormous stomachs in the least bit.

At first Pedro thought the dog would take off after him, but to his surprise, the small four-legged furry creature surprised him yet again, shooting off in the opposite direction yapping loudly for all it was worth. This small window of opportunity allowed Pedro to at least for the moment get the hell out of the path of the rampaging beast.

Pedro quickly found himself running in and out of pockets of thick ground fog now, moving hopefully in the direction back toward the building. He also wondered where his dad was? He had no clue. He had just passed through another thick pocket of fog when he heard something massive moving from somewhere close by. Still keeping his body in motion and refusing to bring himself to a halt, his eyes and head twitched back and forth, searching for the source of the sound through the fog. If he ran right into the massive pillar-sized limbs of one of these creatures that would most certainly be the end of him.

Pedro flung himself around, searching for the source of the sound. He could hear it; smell the foul and offensive odor of the carnivore now. His heart thumped wildly against his small ribcage. Pedro kept his body in motion though. Backtracking through more thick fog, he suddenly slammed straight into something.

***

Davis Brown had located his son. The exhilaration of this, though, was quickly dampened by the perilous situation that they were still in. Davis had heard the boy moving about down here chaotically through the fog, and by the grace of God had been able to locate him, slamming right into him in the process. It was a small miracle in its own right. Now he held his son tight to his chest as though both their lives were hanging in the most precarious of positions. And for all intents and purposes, they were.

Davis looked down at Pedro who had already shown tremendous grit and bravery for coming back down here in the first place. But it was quite evident now that the young boy was visibly shaken. Still though, he was managing to keep it together, managing to put forth a brave face. And for that Davis couldn't have had more respect and admiration for his son.

Not a word was said between the two though, as they remained in a silent embrace. Something was moving from somewhere just off to their left. It was close. And together father and son heard a terrifying sound as air shuddered in and out of a giant chest cavity. They could smell the predator.

They waited and listened.

The creature moved right on by them, the huge mass of it traveling just on the other side of the fog now. They couldn't see the animal, and most importantly it appeared to not be able to see them.

Meanwhile, Davis held them both deathly still, his eyes shifting back and forth. And then to his horror the pockets of fog that had momentarily inundated and blotted out the landscape in a thick blanketing of white, started to thin and dissipate. Out of nowhere the wind had picked up considerably and was now threatening to give up their location. A stiff wind suddenly blew through the area, clearing the last of the ground fog with it.

Time was up. Davis and Pedro now stood fully exposed. Davis caught the tail end of the giant creature as it passed by, only a thin wisp of fog covering a small portion of the huge, muscular tail. And then both Pedro and Davis watched as the huge head turned round and peered down at them. Davis saw the big head, took in the still yet unwavering eyes, and saw the huge rows of teeth as the colossal jaws parted ways. The creature made a low guttural growling sound.

"Run," Pedro whispered to his dad.

Davis and his son took off at a dead sprint in the opposite direction. With the heavy fog having fully cleared, they now had a clear and unobstructed view back to the new construction site.

Now it was a race against time to see if they could get themselves back to the building before the inevitable. Davis thought about swooping Pedro off the ground as he had done before, but felt as though he couldn't spare the time or the loss in momentum. They were both running at top speed now, Davis surprised at his son's sudden burst of speed. All those recesses and PE classes had really done wonders in regard to Pedro's footspeed. Pedro's newfound speed was now on full display as they ran for their lives.

They could hear the creature pounding forward behind them. The crashing sound of all that tonnage pushed them to run even faster. Davis and Pedro had closed to within fifty feet of the building when from somewhere off to their right they heard the faint sound of a dog beginning to bark. It was hard to tell from where the noise was coming, just that the sound was quickly working its way closer to them.

The dog barked louder and louder now. From behind Davis could hear that it appeared as though another one of the towering creatures had joined in the hunt. Davis managed to turn himself around just enough to see that both creatures had momentarily taken an interest in the new yet foreign sound. Bringing his head back around quickly, he knew that this was their chance. They had to get the hell outta here once and for all and get to higher ground.

And that's just what they did, running full bore until finally at long last reaching the opening that led into the building.

26

"Dad, what about the dog?" Pedro shouted as they were now ascending the flights of stairs in great leaps and bounds.

As gut wrenching as it was though, Davis knew that he absolutely could not put both their lives life at risk anymore in order to save the dog. They simply had to get to the top of the building now at all costs. His heart ached for the dog as they continued climbing the stairs.

Davis could only hope and pray that the dog was able to scamper its way to safety. And if safety unfortunately wasn't an option, then he hoped it would end swiftly for the dog and that it wouldn't experience any pain.

They continued climbing the stairs, pushing higher and higher into the building.

Davis saw light streaming in up ahead. They ascended the last flight of stairs and emerged out onto the rooftop of the building.

Davis paused for a moment. The clouds had finally parted ways, which in turn gave way to bright beaming sunlight that shown down brightly atop them all. For a second, Davis remained there as he tried to regain himself, breathing hard, his mind struggling to take it all in. He looked around for a moment trying to gain some clarity. And then all of a sudden, he grabbed hold of Pedro, lifted the boy high into the air, and gave him the biggest hug and kiss imaginable.

Setting Pedro back down on the ground, Davis spoke to his son. "You more than likely saved me back there. Had you not come back down I might have been a goner by now."

Pedro managed somewhat of an awkward smile back. "Yeah but, Dad, I almost got killed too down there. You saved me."

Davis managed a tired smile. "We both saved each other. I say we're even."

By now the rest of the people atop the roof had taken notice of the two and come over to join them. Davis turned to see Elena with a giant smile of relief plastered across her face. The two embraced for a moment with the longest passionate kiss Davis could remember in recent history. Next, he reached down and picked up Ariana and gave her a huge hug and kiss as well.

He set his daughter down on the ground, thankful beyond belief that they were at least safe for the time being. Next Davis saw a powerful and grizzled hand extend itself his way.

"Glad you made it," Pearson said squinting through one eye in the bright sunlight. "Told you to stay close though, but happy to see you're still with us."

Davis managed another smile and reciprocated the handshake. Next Davis and the small group that had gathered by him saw a young man in his early thirties with a baseball cap on quietly approach them.

"You folks, uh, by chance didn't see a dog back

down there on the ground, did you?" Matt Baker asked hesitantly.

Davis felt his heart sink with the question. He shook his head. "We did, but I'm sorry—"

No sooner than Davis had spoken those very words, he was cut off by the sound of a dog barking from what appeared to be somewhere back down in the stairwell. The entire group turned in unison back toward the stairs as the barking grew louder and louder until finally a shape emerged from the dark stairwell and out into the light.

Matt Baker got down on one knee as Hope jumped right into his arms. He engulfed Hope in an enormous bear hug as the mass of the dog literally knocked him to the ground. He continued tickling and scratching Hope as she licked him all over.

Matt turned to the group as he faced the dog in their direction. "I'd like you all to meet Hope."

Davis let out a laugh, which honestly was more relief than joy. As Ariana and Pedro both gathered around his legs, hugging tightly to the lower half of their dad, and Elena put her arm around her husband, the sense of belonging and togetherness that Davis felt for having his family all together and safe at least for the moment, was at an all-time high. Davis leaned over and kissed Elena on the cheek. They were going to get through this ordeal together. They had to. Their future lives together, and all that they would achieve was hinging on them making it out of this alive. Elena was going to make it in Hollywood. She was finally going to break through once and for all and compose soundtracks for big budget Hollywood blockbuster movies. Davis was absolutely certain that this would happen for her as he believed in her talents and abilities one hundred percent. And for himself, he had his podcast *Bullshat* along with the accompanying media company that he intended to launch. Nothing on Earth was going to stand in his way.

Davis thought next about his two precious kids. He wanted their future to be brighter than he had when he was their age. And he would dedicate himself to working hard in his career and family life to make that a reality as well.

Finally, Davis looked over at Matt and Hope, still happy as could be to still be in each other's presence. And then he hugged his family once again, holding them tightly to his body, knowing full well that whatever awaited them, they would face it together, as a family.

***

Commander Gray Pearson managed to put some distance between himself and the rest of the group and had worked his way to the far corner of the rooftop now. The fog had cleared just enough to see all the way back to San Francisco. He could see the iconic city skyline and the tall buildings in the far background. Pearson homed in on the cold blue waters of the San Francisco Bay itself.

And then all of a sudden, the calm and placid waters suddenly began to grow choppy, almost as though something was slowly working its way to the surface. Pearson eyed the water as considerable sized waves began running in all directions now as a monstrous scaly back suddenly materialized and surfaced. Rising what easily had to be several stories out of the water, water ran and flowed down the beast's impenetrable hide in huge cascading waterfalls. It flowed in all directions as the back continued to rise higher and higher out of the water. Pearson remained poised and still, gnawing on a new cigar that he had just wedged tightly into the corner of his mouth.

He watched as the colossal scaled back eventually gave way to the massively powerful crocodilian like tail pushing and torpedoing the huge beast forward like a building-sized submarine. The monstrosity slowly appeared to be surfacing in the same manner as one might expect to see a whale surface. Pearson watched for a few more seconds before just like that the creature submerged and disappeared down into the murky depths below. All that remained now were the choppy, foamy rogue waves running in all directions.

Still gnawing on his new cigar, Pearson felt his blood starting to boil. This creature, if you could even call it that, and its young were responsible for the death of every single one of his men. Squinting against the glare from the sun he continued to eye the water.

"And don't think I've forgotten that," he mumbled to himself. "Don't think I've forgotten that for one second."

The monstrous back of the creature once again became visible through the choppy waves that had now completely overtaken the bay. It appeared to be heading straight for downtown San Francisco now. And it was in that moment that Pearson reassured himself once more that his men had not died in vain on this island. That their lives, and the cause that they had been fully committed to had not been for nothing. They had died for something worthwhile. Pearson vowed to bring every last one of these beasts to their knees if it was the last thing he did on this Earth.

***

With a massive flick of its thick muscled tail, a tail that contained seemingly endless walls of muscles that stacked one atop the next, the leviathan shot itself forward through the water with stunning speed now. As it moved through the water, it was not traveling alone though. Clinging tightly and grasping on everywhere and anywhere there was space upon which to do so onto its untold bulk, the monstrosity carried roughly half a dozen or so of its young atop its back. The young clung to the creature now, using their sharp hooked claws to pierce the tough, crocodilian like hide of their mother. The remainder of them that were still alive had all hitched a ride from Yerba Buena Island, and now set their sights on a much bigger target—downtown San Francisco.

The giant continued torpedoing through the water. Like crocodilians, it was able to stay under water submerged for a good amount of time before finally needing air. Eventually though it would need to come up for air, as both it and its young were only semi-aquatic.

The monster produced another powerful flick of its tail and again sent itself shooting through the shallows, sending up huge waves on all sides of it. It was now moving like one might expect to see a crocodile or alligator propelling their body through the water. The only real difference being the staggering size disparity. To this leviathan, even a twenty-foot-long salt-water crocodile would seem but a mere ant in terms of size and scale. Absolutely nothing on this planet could match it.

The monster glided effortlessly through the water for several hundred more feet before finally its cavernous lungs sent the message to its brain. It was time to breathe. The young needed to breathe as well. With thoughts of oxygen in mind as well as making its way up and onto dry land, the creature rose up and lifted its enormous bulk from the water. It was an awe inspiring, surreal sight to see the thing stand up right there in the middle of the San Francisco Bay, water falling and cascading down all sides of its staggering mass as it lifted itself higher and higher into the air. An earth-shattering roar heralded the creature having finally risen to its full height. The giant head adorned with two protruding horns the size of small trees now towered some three hundred feet above the water, absolutely dwarfing everything in sight.

For a moment the creature simply stood there in silence, its two enormous feet planted down firmly in the soft squishy mud that made up the bottom of the San Francisco Bay, the huge-spiked tail stretched out behind the body swaying back and forth rhythmically. Its oversized front clawed forelimbs dangled over the water. During the journey through the water, its young had been momentarily displaced. Many of them now clung tightly on all fours from new locations on their mother's body, their own forms soaking wet and glistening in the late afternoon sun.

As the limbs of the monster suddenly started to come to life once again, huge waves were displaced and pushed out in all directions. It continued moving, the tall waves rising up on all sides of its limbs as it walked through the water. The massive, clawed feet continued sloshing their way forward through the silty bottom.

Meanwhile, perched high atop various locations and clinging tightly to the animal, a half a dozen or so of its young each let out heralding cries of their own. Using all four of their limbs, the young gripped and dug in wherever they could with sharp, oversized claws.

And then, in one final act of dominance and aggression, the monster let loose a thunderous rumbling cry, the noise reverberating out across the landscape. The creature continued moving forward toward the high-rise buildings that made up downtown San Francisco. It wouldn't be long now until it officially made landfall.

www.PrimalPublishing.com

twitter.com/MichaelEsola

CHECK OUT THESE OTHER PREHISTORIC THRILLERS BY MICHAEL ESOLA

APEX

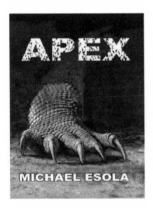

Two young and determined entrepreneurs set out to create an annual convention called Prehistoric Con. What was supposed to be a glorious evening in celebration of all things prehistoric—showcasing bestselling authors, movie directors, executive producers, screenwriters, and a host of others from the industry—takes a sudden turn for the worst with the reality that they have been locked inside the building with no way out. It isn't long before the entire convention comes to the horrifying realization that they are being hunted, and that from the dark places within the building, things are starting to stir to life.

PREHISTORIC

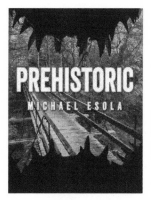

A giant boardwalk has been resurrected high up in the Indonesian rainforest canopy, offering guests stunning, spectacular, and unparalleled views of the rainforest. However, the boardwalk is incomplete and in need of more funding. The creator, John Corstine, assembles a group of potential investors for a weekend tour of the boardwalk. Little do they know that high up in the rainforest canopy, they are being watched, but more importantly, they are not alone.

HYBRID

Fresh off an expedition to the wilds of Indonesia, Bick Downs returns home to his beloved San Francisco. It isn't long before he learns that an ancient species of predator has been released and is running amok in the city. He joins forces with others in an attempt to capture the mysterious creature, only to learn that up north, in the sleepy agricultural town of Santa Rosa, California, something even more terrifying and sinister has been created

PRIMAL

Bick Downs and the Society of Cryptozoological Agents are dropped into the lush bamboo forests of Vietnam. They are searching for Gigantopithecus, the largest primate that has ever existed. But what they find deep and entangled amongst the trees is not the reclusive giant that roamed the bamboo forests of Southeast Asia several million years ago. Instead, they find something else entirely. The animal has evolved.

SILVERBACK

A man wakes at dawn in order to get in an early morning run. Quietly, he climbs over a fallen tree that blocks the secluded dirt trail. As he slowly begins his run, unbeknownst to him, he is being watched. For inside the dense foliage and creeping ivy, the forest is very much alive.

THE ICE GORILLA

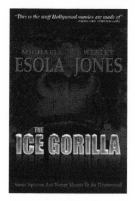

A group of researchers travel to the Arctic in search of a mysterious claw. The ice shelf they are conducting research on suddenly breaks away from the mainland. They find themselves trapped on a floating island of ice and come to the horrifying realization that they are not alone.